Uncultured PEARL

by

Sherrill M. LEWIS

Book One
Maggie Storm Blue Mystery

Shoppe Foreman Publishing

Guthrie, Oklahoma, USA

Published by

Shoppe Foreman Publishing

3507 Homesteaders Lane
Guthrie, Oklahoma 73044 USA
www.ShoppeForeman.com

cover watercolor by Bill Miller
Stillwater, Oklahoma

Printed in the United States of America
Printing/manufacturing information
can be found on the last page.

ISBN-13: 978-1500605216
ISBN-10: 1500605212

Acknowledgements

I thank God for the joy derived from the many talents with which he has blessed his child, assuring that I am rarely bored. I'm grateful for the birthmother who chose life for me, and the adopted grandparents who unselfishly raised me.

My gratitude extends to my patient husband, Gene, who came up with a *curriculum vita* for Rod Richardson that seemed more complete than my own life story.

Without the tireless assistance of many re-reads and edits by Judith Sexton, Robert Parks, and several other members of the Stillwater Writers, this book would never have come to life. Lt. Kyle Gibbs, Stillwater Police Department, patiently and thoroughly answered questions on police procedural questions. Bill Miller, a very talented artist, created the cover artwork. My intrepid publisher, Larry Foreman, walked me through the mystifying world of publishing a novel. Thank you, one and all!

The characters and local events are fictional products of the author's overactive imagination. The names of the guilty and innocent have been changed, or used fictionally, to protect them and the author. Baysinger Cove and Baywater County exist only in Maggie's world.

Table of Contents

Chapter	Title	Page
1	Maggie Arrives in Maine	1
2	Maggie Winds Down	13
3	Watcher Knows Death Becomes You	25
4	Pattysue Morgan Is Safe	29
5	Pattysue Hears News Red and Prose Purple	37
6	Maggie Hears the News	44
7	Maggie Meets Baby and Friends	46
8	Maggie Considers Angels and Fools	55
9	Maggie Enjoys Food, Faith, and Friendship	62
10	Maggie Reminisces	66
11	Maggie, It's Shindig Time!	77
12	Maggie Meets Strangers	87
13	Maggie Sees Fireworks and Sparks	92
14	Maggie Sees More Sparks	98
15	Maggie Finds a Clue	115
16	Maggie Travels the Dusty Backstreets of Memory	121
17	Maggie Wades through Sticky Thickets	124
18	Maggie Finds a Lull in the Storm?	135
19	Maggie Faces a Dilemma	142

20	Maggie Hears Ring-Ding-Ding	145
21	Who Sends a Pocketfull of Posies?	147
22	Jobina's Anniversary!	149
23	Maggie's Goin' Dancing Tonight	152
24	Maggies Two-Steppin' Blues	154
25	Maggie at the Church Picnic	160
26	Maggie Hears Rod's Story	166
27	Maggie: Shop, Shop, Click	170
28	Maggie Plays Whodunit	175
29	Maggie Talks of Wishes and Horses	184
30	Maggie Finds S-S-Sweets, My Sweet?	192
31	Maggie, Whatcha Think?	201
32	Maggie Goes Sleuthing!	209
33	Pattysue, Just Once More	215
34	Maggie Faces a Confrontation	221
35	Maggie Sees Pictures Worth Many Tears	226
36	Carrie, It's a Done Deal	237
37	Maggie, *Vaya con Dios*	246
38	Maggie Has a Revelation	256
	Pearls	262
	The Author	264

1

Maggie Arrives in Maine

Sunday, June 24th, early afternoon

"IF I WERE MARRIED TO A MAN who did that to me, I'd be a widow," Maggie Storm Blue stated. She was watching a young mother and a squirming toddler standing at the cafe's bakery takeout counter. The child stood on tiptoes with her nose pressed against the glass. A large cartoon-emblazoned bandage dwarfed the little girl's rosebud cheek. The woman under Maggie's intense scrutiny wore a cast on her right arm and sported a rainbow-hued left eye.

Maggie, along with her Aunt Larkin and Uncle Rod Richardson, were in the front foyer of the Sawmill Hill Cafe, waiting to be seated.

"I do declare, Maggie, that is a drastic statement," Larkin replied, her Georgia-born drawl smoothing out the syllables.

"It sure looks like spousal abuse to me."

"I wonder what she'll do now." Rod moved out of the way of people leaving the cafe. The door admitted a quick blast of hot, humid air before it whooshed shut.

"Pattysue!" Larkin beckoned to the young woman. "Come over here, dear, there's someone I want you to meet."

Pattysue dropped the change into her purse. "Be right there."

Larkin made the introductions then laid her hand on Pattysue's cast. "Mercy, whatever happened to you and little Kaleen?"

"M-my h-husband. Drunk." Her soft voice changed to steel. "Bob's not going to hurt us ever again."

"I surely do hope you are feeling better soon," Larkin said, exuding sympathy.

"Thanks, Mrs. Richardson."

Pattysue was fast losing ground in an awkward attempt to control the slippery bakery box while her squiggling child tugged on her skirt.

"What are your plans?" Rod asked.

"We're staying in Willow Grove with my sister, for now. We came back today to get some things we needed. Kaleen loves Paw-Paw's cookies, so we had to stop here first, of course."

Peeking around her mother's legs, Kaleen looked up at Maggie. "We got cookies with sprinkles. I like sprinkles."

"I like sprinkles, too, especially chocolate ones." Maggie smiled at the cherubic face wreathed in smiles.

"Oh, I almost forgot! The mystery books you ordered came in, Mr. Richardson. Harold is holding them for you at the bookstore." She shrugged. "I can't work for a while yet."

The bakery box started to slip. A passing waitress deftly caught it and slid it into a paper bag with handles.

Pattysue smiled her thanks. Glancing down at her daughter, she said, "Come, Kaliebug, let's go."

Dancing two steps ahead of her mother, Kaleen's fluffy golden-red curls kept time with every hop, bop, and skip.

A horn-rim-spectacled man held the door open for them.

"Later 'gator!" he said to Kaleen.

"After 'while, croc'dile," she sang out, followed by a high-pitched giggle.

"First table's open. Take a seat, folks. I'll be right there with coffee." The waitress tossed the comment over her shoulder and hurried toward the kitchen.

Dodging the tendrils of a low-hanging plant, Maggie leaned sideways on the red vinyl bench seat, trying to see between the spots on the rain-spattered window. "Dratted Boston fern," she fussed, brushing away the too-friendly frond tickling her face. She watched Pattysue and Kaleen ease their way into the back seat of a mid-size car idling in the parking lot.

Maggie turned to face her relatives. "I really don't understand why women put up with abuse. Fear, I suppose, though victims have more options nowadays."

The waitress was fast approaching with a full pot of steaming coffee. Maggie flipped the white ceramic mug upright, ready for the incoming brew.

"I'll be back in a jiff to take your orders." The waitress slapped menus on the table and sloshed coffee into their mugs without spilling a drop.

Maggie took a cautious sip of the hot coffee. The aromatic steam bathed her face and fogged up her glasses. "Ahhhh."

"Oh, Maggie, I'm so glad you're here, finally!" her aunt exclaimed, running a manicured nail down the Senior Delights section of the menu.

"Me, too." Maggie sighed a breath of relief. "I've been under so much stress lately, I couldn't wait to hop on that plane. My boss was not at all happy. Because a doctor was adamant about my taking a full month's leave, Mrs. Allgood had no choice but to comply."

Rod spooned ice out of his water glass and dropped the chips into his steaming coffee. "We're glad to have you here. It's been way too long since we last got together."

The heady aroma of coffee clashed with the distinctive smell of Juicy Fruit gum. The waitress topped off their mugs. "You ready now?" She steadied her order pad, one knee resting on the bench seat next to Maggie. "Heather" was embroidered in purple on the pocket of her pink blouse. So totally in character and reflecting the cafe's retro theme.

Heather, gum a-snapping, headed toward the kitchen with their orders.

Larkin leaned forward. "Where were we? Oh, yes. I want to know all about Kenneth. Have you two set a date yet?"

"Hardly that. Without even an apology, Kenneth announced that he was moving to New York to marry somebody named Virgil, of all things!" Exasperated, she lapsed into a cliché. "There's no one else lurking in the wings, either."

"Well, really!" Larkin's Southern molasses accent dripped with indignation. Her slight scowl emphasized the crinkles caused by years of more mirth than misery.

"Didn't you have a clue about his persuasion?" Rod asked.

"Nope, nary a one," Maggie answered, twirling a wavy lock of silver-threaded black hair. "Anyway, I've given up on men. Pretty much decided I'll be single for the rest of my life."

"You're sure now?" Larkin's finely formed white eyebrows rose in full flight.

"Yes, I'm fine with it. Resigned, you might say."

"Well, since you've given over, now God has a chance to work in your life," Larkin said, nodding with conviction.

"Hrumpf."

"Maggie, dear, when you get out of His way, He can work."

Maggie pushed a wayward strand of hair behind her ear. "We'll see."

Rod patted his wife's hand. "Hmm, Larkin, m'love, what about my friend, Wayne Hardy? He's a nice guy."

He smiled across the table at Maggie. "He owns Hardy Hardware. We'll invite him over so you can meet him."

"Whoa! Please don't bother." Maggie remembered her manners. "Thank you, though. I'm exhausted. I need my spiritual and personal batteries recharged. I'm only here for a few weeks, anyway. A long-distance relationship is doomed before it begins."

"It's no bother, Maggie, dear. When you move back here, there will be no 'long distance' about it!" Larkin looked smug, like she had just solved *that* little problem, thank you very much. She took a drink of the cooling coffee and wrinkled her nose.

Maggie's doting relatives had been urging her for the past year to "come back home." Ten days ago, Maggie had called her aunt. During their lengthy conversation, she mentioned her upcoming doctor-mandated time off. Vickie Blake, one of her best friends, was a doctor. She had noted Maggie's alarming level of stress. Concerned about her friend's emotional and psychic health, Vickie wrote a Leave of Absence order and insisted that Maggie submit it forthwith. It was not to forestall a nervous breakdown, but to encourage her to refocus her life and goals, far away from the contentious issues bombarding her.

Larkin had invited her niece to spend most of that time with them in Maine. It hadn't taken much convincing. Maggie agreed to come, just as soon as she could get her ducks lined up.

Drifting from the cafe's kitchen were the tantalizing smells of bacon sizzling on the grill, potatoes popping in hot oil, and coffee burbling its fresh finale. Maggie's stomach rumbled. The yogurt she had bolted down for breakfast in Oklahoma was a distant memory, along with the granola bars she had munched on while flying somewhere over green pastures.

"What is keeping our meals?" she asked, rubbing her temples in an attempt to ease the hunger-driven headache. "I'm starved."

Heather walked up with an apologetic smile for Maggie. "Sorry, I forgot, like, what you ordered?"

"It is number thirty-eight. Think of it as an age you won't be for a long time." Maggie paused, removed her glasses, ran her hand down her face and grimaced. "I'm sorry, Heather. I didn't mean to snap at you."

Heather blushed all the way to her naturally impossible shade of rocket-fire red hair and rushed toward the kitchen.

A few minutes later, their meals were on the table. Rod said grace then shook tableware out of his napkin. "Come on, let's eat."

Maggie was delighted to discover that her BLT was built on dense wheat bread, home-baked, fresh and thick-sliced, which wouldn't soggy down when heaped with mayo. The bacon was crispy, and the tomato, garden fresh.

"Remember when we picked you up from the airport, I said the food here was good? You fussed about the two-hour drive, but don't you agree that it was worth waiting for?"

"Umhum," Maggie mumbled with her mouth full. She swallowed and picked up a pickle. "Now, what's the story on Pattysue?"

"I am just sick about them," Larkin said between bites of her tuna melt sandwich. "This is not the first time Robert Morgan has taken a swing at Pattysue. He's never hurt little Kaleen before, though."

"News travels fast in a small town." Rod swirled a French fry in a puddle of ketchup.

Maggie picked up her coffee mug. "No great surprise, that."

"Pattysue's maternal grandmother, Patricia, is a quilter friend of mine," Larkin said. "She told me about two previous incidents."

"Third time's the charm, eh? Sounds like Pattysue *will* leave him this time. Bob Morgan is a regular Jekyll-and-Hyde type." Rod bit into his double cheeseburger. He swallowed and wiped his mouth with a napkin. "A real charmer when he's sober and pure-d despicable when he's got an edge-on." Rod's natural Yankee-speak pronounced it *aidge*-on.

"Jekyll? Jerk is more like it." Maggie ditched her fork in favor of using fingers to grasp the crispy French fries. "If ever a man pitched me even a modicum of malicious mayhem, I'd consider malevolency."

* * * * *

"Come along, dear." Larkin linked her arm in Maggie's as they walked together to the car. "I am so glad the sun has finally shone his face. Let's head for home. I imagine you're plum tuckered out after that long flight."

Maggie acknowledged that she was tired indeed. "You can always tell I'm exhausted when I slip into florid purple prose."

Rod turned left out of the cafe's parking lot onto Morrilton Road. Minutes later he made a right turn, heading south on Franklin Road. A large colorful sign greeted them: *Welcome to Baysinger Cove ~ Idyllic Retreat Betwixt the Mountain, Lakes, and Sea.*

Donning a figurative Tour Guide hat, Larkin explained the town's slogan. "Our little town is bordered by Serenadelle Lake, Horseshoe Lake, Old Man Mountain, and the Atlantic Ocean. Not too long ago it was teetering on the brink of becoming a ghost town. Back then, with its hundredth birthday approaching, the Town Council decided that our little town was worth saving."

"Nothing like a common goal to inspire people," Rod agreed.

They passed by Reel It In, the fishing supply and bait shop. Rod slightly lifted his index finger from the steering wheel in a non-verbal Yankee greeting to the man standing near the road. Typical for the area's seafaring industry, the old man was decked out in full fishing gear.

"Everyone loves a party, so the townspeople rolled up their collective sleeves to paint, prune, and plant," Larkin continued. "Even folks who didn't know a weed from a wisteria got in the spirit of things. Our mayor, bless her Yankee heart, badgered the Town Council into hiring a marketing strategist. Baysinger Cove is now a tourist destination, not a detour."

The vista was balm for Maggie's weary spirit. Each house and cottage, middle-aged, ancient, or dandy, sat on its plot of terra firma with dignity and pride. Front yards showcased flower gardens ranging from reserved to riotous. Wildflowers, tickled by the warm June breeze, created a giggle of color. Elegant birches, their gray-white bark shimmering in the slanting sunlight, swayed in a graceful dance with the red-brown cedars and blue-green spruces.

Rod slowed for the busy traffic crossing ahead. A full-cheeked chipmunk, with his squirrel buddy right on his tail, skittered across the street. Overhead, a raucous blue jay made a strafing run in a swirl of blue feathers. *Le soleil,* making a valiant attempt to dispel scudding clouds, was on his slow daily journey westward.

"Many years ago, the railroad served an important part of everyday life. Now, a cooperative of local artists has taken over the train station. They call it Art at the Depot," Larkin said. "If you'd like to, we might visit there sometime while you're here."

"Sounds very interesting. I would like that." Maggie looked back and forth, trying to take in the whole town all at once. "But what on earth is that?"

That was one of the oddest houses Maggie had ever seen.

Three A-frames had been joined, slightly overlapping. "It looks weird."

"Sometime in the late sixties, an architect built it for his own home. Bit odd looking, but then Rich Drury always was a mite tetched," Rod answered.

"It would make an interesting shop."

Stuck on a post in the front lawn, the sign announced: Coming Soon! Fine Feathers – Her Haberdashery.

"Our ever-efficient news-vine, in the person of Birdie Mandrill, said that Fredericka Larkspur intends to have a slightly upscale, casual clothing store. She hopes to be open by early autumn," Larkin explained. "Which reminds me, we're going to Freddi's daughter's baby shower this coming Saturday morning."

"*We* are?" Maggie was amused by Larkin's automatic inclusion of her in local activities.

"Of course. The minute I knew you were coming I accepted for both of us."

Maggie noticed a jaunty sign swinging on its post. "Fun store names," she exclaimed, distracted from her aunt's self-assured comment. "Suds Ye Duds, Paperwhite, Hair Doux. Any special reason?"

"The Town Council wanted to emphasize the old town's charm. They took a page from Aspen's cutesy shop names."

Maggie remembered the vacation she had spent with her relatives in Aspen, Colorado, one summer ten years ago. That was the last time they had all been together. Time: mercurial and fleeting, and as tangible as fairy dust.

"Look at that one – it looks like a barn with saddlebags." The saddlebag effect was created by a saltbox-style addition tacked on each side of the gambrel-roofed main house. "If it were painted green, it would look like a giant frog."

Larkin laughed. "Yes, it would! It's our Community Events Center. Among other things, it's a community playhouse. We hold dances, concerts, craft shows, and all sorts of other events there."

"The Happy Bookworm — oh, joyful news, a bookstore! That's great! And a candy shop," she said, spying the sign for Sweet Things. "Books and chocolate. Great combination, that."

A few minutes later, they came to Loon Creek Road and turned left. Less than a hundred yards further, Rod slowed to make the tight right-hand turn onto Richardson Lane.

"Hey! A road named after you? How cool is that?"

Her uncle chuckled. "That's what happens when you own the whole clambake."

Rod drove slower, passing under a wrought iron arch. *Eagles' Rest* was written in flowing iron cursive between the curves of the arch. The gates stood open at right angles to the very tall wrought iron fences leading off to the east and west. Tall pine trees bracketed the long, wide, paved driveway, tamping the road noise down to a muffled hum.

"Those eight-foot-tall fences create an effective barrier to discourage intruders. They also mark the north side property line. We're on a ten-acre deep peninsula into Horseshoe Lake. Each fence stops right at the edge of the lake." As he traveled around a gentle curve, the massive log house came into view.

"Wow, oh wow! The pictures you sent didn't do it justice. It's awesome!"

2

Maggie Winds Down

June 24th, late afternoon

ONE OF THE TWO DOUBLEWIDE DOORS of the over-sized four-car garage rose. Rod parked the BMW between a Voyager van and a Jeep Wrangler. Maggie almost fell off the back seat in her excitement.

"I would like to think that you being a wordsmith, child, you could manage a grander word or two," Larkin scolded in a mock-serious tone. She opened the door leading to a spacious utility room and waited for Maggie to join her.

"It's simply fabulous." Maggie ran out of adjectives and paused for breath. "Why the name, Uncle Rod? Are there eagles here?"

"I'm retired from the Air Force, as you know." He took Maggie's small purple carry-on suitcase out of the trunk. "A pair of bald eagles has a nest in a huge old tree on the far eastside shoreline, on the mountain side of Horseshoe Lake."

Larkin led Maggie into the kitchen while Rod took the suitcase up to the guest suite by way of the garage stairs. Frantic barks increased in volume. A blur of black and white fur barreled around the corner, skidded on the tile floor, and stopped right at Larkin's feet. The dog's furry tail thumped the floor in double-quick time as her front paws tapped a polka.

"She's a Border Collie, so she'll try to herd you." Larkin reached down to pet the dog. "Hello, Sheba. This is Maggie. Be nice."

Sheba moved over to sniff Maggie's shoes. Maggie scratched the soft ears and greeted the dog. Her curiosity apparently satisfied about this tall stranger, Sheba trotted toward the door in a jig-dancing bid for outdoor time, with Larkin close behind.

Out of the corner of her eye, Maggie caught a movement just above her head. "By the way, Aunt Larkin, who is the ornamental piece on top of the fridge?"

Larkin laughed. "That's Siam. He's a Siamese-Tabby mix, a little over a year old but still very kittenish. We got him and Sheba both, oh, about six months ago from the Orphan Paws Rescue in Moose Valley. Siam is Mr. Personality and will become your best friend if you give him the least bit of attention."

Maggie wandered around the kitchen, and Larkin changed subjects. "If you like to cook, Maggie, there's plenty left to do for our annual July Fourth Shindig. I do hope Mother Nature cooperates again this year. So far, every year we've been blessed with reasonably good weather."

Sheba barked once. Larkin let her in, and the dog woofed her thanks.

"Go to your basket, Sheba," Larkin said, walking out of the kitchen with Maggie.

Sheba jumped into a large sheepskin-lined basket tucked under the baby grand piano. Her liquid brown eyes were watchful as she peered over the wicker edge. Siam, a gray blur right on Sheba's heels, hopped into the basket and proceeded to lick the dog's ears.

"We call this the Lake Room because of the outstanding view of Horseshoe Lake. That's Old Man Mountain there on the far side of the lake."

Old Man Mountain consisted of craggy lumps and chunks of granite freckled with leafy green trees, and bearded with tall bushes hugging the steep incline. At the base of the mountain, Horseshoe Lake kissed the chunky gravel-strewn embankment. The wind was freshening, ruffling the boughs of the fir trees.

The waves and ripples tickled the foot of the mountain, the cold blue water giggling into lacy froth. Floating effortlessly, mallard ducks rode the roller-coaster waves and danced on the whitecaps. Some, with feathery butts up and webbed feet waving, were diving for their dinners.

"It's far grander than any great room I've ever seen," Maggie answered, her green eyes wide with admiration. She scanned the view framed by bay windows that went all the way up to the pine tongue-and-groove bead-board ceiling.

"I never realized until this minute how much I have missed living around here. It's really bad when the stink of low tide causes me to wax nostalgic." She rotated her head, loosening the crick in her neck. "We don't get that in land-locked Oklahoma."

"You do have lakes there. Quite a few, if I remember correctly."

"Yes, but they are all man-made. When I discovered that, I felt like I'd been cheated somehow. I suppose a lake's a lake, regardless how it came about."

Larkin rested her hand on the peeled-cedar support post at the foot of the two-flight staircase. The base of the satin-finished post included some of the tree's top roots.

How novel, Maggie thought.

"You're in the guest suite upstairs. I unpacked the boxes you sent and hung up the clothes, but I left the rest for you to take care of as you wish."

"Thank you."

Larkin placed her hands on Maggie's shoulders and gathered her niece into a warm hug. "Child, it has been too many years. I still can't quite take it in that you are really here."

Returning the hug, Maggie noticed how frail her aunt seemed. Pulling away, her voice wavered. "I know. Neither can I. It *has* been way too long. Thank you for convincing me to come."

"You are always welcome." Larkin took a delicate pink hankie out of her sleeve. "It's been a long day, dear, so we'll sit for a spell. You go find a comfy chair, and I'll get us some iced peach tea." Lifting up silver-rimmed glasses, she wiped her eyes and turned toward the kitchen.

"Un-sweet, please," Maggie called after her.

She walked around, taking a gradual survey of the Lake Room. In front of the tall bay windows, a baby grand piano was silhouetted against the backdrop of Horseshoe Lake and the mountain. Near the piano's gentle curve, two guitars were propped in heavy wrought iron stands. To the left of the windows, a full-wall, built-in bookcase stopped short of the ceiling. A rolling ladder provided access to the elusive upper shelves. Two ceiling fans moved the air with a lazy hum.

A magnificent polished-fieldstone fireplace dominated the opposite wall. Hanging in pride of place above the elaborately carved oak mantel was a large, framed photograph of an eagle in full flight. Handwritten in silver ink, words in a dramatic scrawl across the lower face of the black suede mat read: *"They who wait for the Lord will renew their strength; they will mount up on wings of eagles."* In the lower left corner of the photograph were the artist's initials: CJD.

"Isaiah 40:31," Rod said, walking toward her. "My favorite verse."

Maggie turned and faced him. Gray hair and mustache set comfortably in a face worn leather-wrinkly by sun, wind, and time. Gold-rimmed glasses framed his jade green eyes. He stood six-foot-two, just as straight and trim now as he was on the day he saluted a Major General at the Pentagon. Though he was on the leeward side of eighty years old, he was still a handsome man.

Maggie noted the absence of the ubiquitous television that dominates living rooms and discourages conversations. "What, no TV?" she asked, surprised, thinking she was the only person in America without one.

"We gave it up right before we moved to North Belgrade, seven years ago. We lived there for two years while this house was being built. Here, we much prefer the awesome views, or reading. We both grew tired of the inane offerings Hollywood dishes up. Everything they do is under the specious premise of good entertainment."

Specious? Ah, yes: misleading. Maggie recalled that her uncle was a voracious reader, a worker of complex

16

crossword puzzles, and often used what her English teacher had called "ten dollar words." Aunt Larkin, a literary wizard, was a collector of old, obscure, and uncommonly used words. Maggie, also a reader and a wordsmith, wondered if it was a family eccentricity or a personal idiosyncrasy.

"We've always liked some of the old movies, though," Rod conceded.

"I like them, too. I don't have a TV either, for many of the same reasons. Haven't had one, well, it's been over thirty years now."

"In the media room upstairs," he waved his hand in that general direction, "we have a DVD player and a large movie screen. Comfortable seats, of course, and a genuine old-timey popcorn maker, too."

They claimed the oversized club chairs situated in front of the bookcase wall. Larkin favored one of the two wing-backed chairs facing them. A basket of needlework lay at her feet. The seriousness of the tall task lamp was discreetly camouflaged by a matte black shade. Larkin tipped it slightly, angling the light onto the work in her lap. She stitched while Rod and Maggie chattered away about their favorite movies.

Rod preferred John Wayne and old war movies. Maggie's favorites were anything with Cary Grant, Spencer Tracy, or Katharine Hepburn. She made a mental note to check out her uncle's DVD library. A John Wayne extravaganza set would be a good Christmas gift for him, if he didn't already have it.

"Who all's been invited to your Shindig? Or perhaps it would be quicker to ask, who have you *not* invited?" Due to conflicting activities, Maggie had yet to visit Baysinger Cove or attend the annual party. "I'm glad I get to be here for it this year."

"We are, too, dear. Like I said earlier, I'll appreciate your help."

"Not a problem."

"Considering that our little town is blessed with about a thousand souls, maybe half the town!" Larkin's laughter lent a grace note to the silvery tinkle of a wind chime hanging outside the kitchen window. "Folks consider it a real honor to receive a formal invitation from us. I send those out to special people and dignitaries, like the mayor. Others, I call or e-mail. They and their extended families all seem to show up.

"Sheriff Walker Bainbridge and his wife Abigail always come. She owns the Snippets quilt shop. The Quilt Society meets there on first Fridays. Our good friend, CJ Dubois, is a Texas transplant. The Davidsbys, they own the Sawmill Hill Cafe, most of their clan come, of course."

She named several other prominent townspeople, none of whom Maggie recognized except from casual mention in Larkin's frequent letters.

"Our mayor and her family will be here. She is a crazy quilter and one of my Sewing Circle ladies."

"Please tell me you didn't invite Marion's other three daughters," Maggie begged. "My erstwhile sisters," she elaborated with heavy sarcasm.

Larkin glanced at her niece before answering. "It's been donkey's years since we've heard anything about your sisters. It seems like they dropped off the face of the earth after Marion's funeral. I shouldn't say it, but that's no great loss."

"After our mother died, they went to live with Aunt June. Oh, bless 'em! They got to grow up with odious Cousin Victor. Please say you didn't invite him, either."

"Wouldn't do. But people do tend to drop in, regardless."

The sun gave up the ghost for this day. Soft lights came on in the Lake Room. Maggie looked up in surprise.

"Automatic," Rod said. "Just like the headlights in the car. The control panel is over there, above the stereo deck."

At the far left side of the towering bookcase wall, a six-foot-high pony wall was offset at a forty-five-degree angle. It had built-in cabinets boasting an elaborate stereo system. A full complement of CDs, cassette tapes, and records were stored on shelves designed especially to accommodate them. Set in the wall directly above the stereo deck was a panel full of a bewildering array of switches, knobs, and blinking lights. It reminded Maggie of the control deck of a fantasy starship.

Raking long ring-bedecked fingers through her travel-ruffled hair, Maggie said, "Funny how certain things trigger memories. I must have been about fifteen, I guess. Grandfather had picked me up after school. While waiting at a traffic light, I said, 'There is no little man in there!' He replied, chuckling, ''Bout time you figured that out.' When I was wee small, I had asked him what made the lights change. He told me that a little man lived up there, making the magic."

Dreaming doggy dramas, Sheba snuffled and shifted in her basket, upsetting the cat draped immodestly across her back. Siam adjusted himself then curled up spoon-fashion with his back against the dog's stomach. A few minutes later, Siam leaped out of the basket, stretched, and sauntered over by Larkin's chair.

Maggie stretched and stifled a yawn. "Three glorious weeks here. Can you put up with me for that long? You sure?" She picked up the L.L.Bean catalog from the side table.

"It's more like: can you put up with us old folks? So far, we can keep up with the best of 'em!" Rod answered.

"From your letters and e-mails, it sounds like your job is interesting, but reading between the lines, you're not happy." Larkin put the crazy quilt block she had been working on into the basket and shut the lid before Siam could jump in.

Maggie closed the catalog. "Good ol' Allgood Advertising Agency. I love the work but not my job, if that makes any sense. I'm having major issues now with the rampant nepotism that has recently arrived in the person of Elbert Allgood." Maggie twisted a lock of hair, a dead giveaway that she was aggrieved.

"Delbert Allgood hired his wife's favorite nephew, Elbert. Without even a 'by your leave,' Mrs. Allgood installed a second desk in my office. Elbert's music choice of hard rock, maxed out on bass and volume, is beyond annoying when I'm trying to write finicky copy. He refused to turn the volume down, so I unplugged the radio, which caused no end of a rumpus," Maggie said with an impish smile. "Of course, Mrs. A said that it was *my* error in judgment. However, she did condescend to tell the Brat to turn it way down. I am sorely tempted to pitch the radio in the dumpster. Wouldn't like to have the cleaning people blamed for it, though."

"And they surely would be blamed," Larkin agreed.

"If I leave the room, when I return, Elbert is installed at the computer checking his emails, surfing the web, and playing games – the lazy bum. The latest donnybrook happened a few weeks ago. I was on deadline for a major project. When I asked him to give it over, Elbert-Brat smirked and said, 'Make me.'"

Rod smoothed his mustache but failed to hide his grin. "What did you do then?"

"Unplugged it," Maggie said, matching his grin. She sipped tea before taking up her saga again. "Then I stormed into Mrs. Allgood's office. I told her, as politely as I could with my teeth gritted, what was going on. I proposed that the company either purchase a second computer or fire Elbert. She called my actions insubordination. I called it insurrection, and told her so. She put a reprimand in my personnel file."

Maggie grimaced and rolled her eyes. "The reprimand didn't bother me as much as her despotic attitude. She even had the audacity to suggest I bring my personal laptop to work. Like *that* would ever happen! Short of full-fledged mutiny, and standing on principle, I refused. Meanwhile, when not fighting with the Brat, I have to pander to the superciliously egotistical demands of certain clients with more money than sense and an alarming lack of manners. Some days I just want …" Maggie paused, indulging in another stretch.

"Just want to give over?" Larkin finished, using a

Southernism.

"Yes, I aim to, someday," she concurred, holding forth with another yawn. "I'd quit in a picosecond. But there are promises to keep yet," she said with her usual stoicism. "I could move on, but getting another job would be much harder now that I'm in my fifties. No matter what anyone says to the contrary, in today's job market, age *does* matter."

She tried to stifle another yawn and failed. "Jobs aren't that thick on the ground in the Oklahoma City metro area, at least not ones I want to do, or can do."

"Changing jobs does not mean the problems change, just the faces," Larkin observed. "You cannot run away because you always take *yourself* with you."

"Quite true, Auntie. Too true." She covered her mouth with both hands to hide yet one more yawn.

"You'd best turn in. It's late. For the last hour you've been gawping like a pelican getting ready to feed." Rod gathered up their empty tea glasses.

"We'll go shopping tomorrow, right after breakfast, or whatever you ladies want to do. I'll chauffeur. While we're out, m'love, we'd better pick up the decorations for the Shindig. It'll be on us before we know it." He headed for the kitchen.

Beyond the French doors dressed in ecru lace curtains, Maggie was transported to an earlier time period in the guest suite. Her aunt had owned a thriving high-end antique store in Georgia. The décor of this room certainly proved that Larkin knew her stuff. Elegant Victoriana, including the tall, canopied four-poster bed set on the diagonal in the soft mauve-painted bedroom. Maggie turned full circle, taking in the room's gentle ambiance.

"Lovely, Aunt Larkin, just right!" Eyelids at half-mast, she had an overwhelming urge to dive head first into the downy softness and not come up for air until Christmas.

Trees whispered a night song. Languid waves caressed the lakeshore. Sheba barked. A loon cried. Maggie yawned.

Tomorrow. I'm tired. I'll think about it tomorrow. "Just call me Scarlett," she said to her reflection in the gold-framed oval mirror. She hung up the pink towel and slipped into her nightgown. Stumbling up the three-step stair, she fell gratefully onto the downy-deep pillow-top mattress.

Whatcha gonna do, Maggie Storm Blue?

Her handsome husband, guitarist and songwriter Kiernan Irish Blue, in the early months of their all-too-short marriage, had written a love song for her. One week before the end of his second tour of Vietnam, Kiernan returned home with a Purple Heart and a flag-draped casket.

The haunting melody and the tag line ran through her mind whenever she faced a hard decision, was in a dilemma, or was discouraged.

With her head snuggled down in the soft pillow, she did not entertain another thought until the Monday morning sun crept between the lace curtains and kissed her nose.

3

Watcher Knows Death Becomes You

Tuesday, June 26th, late night

TWO DAYS LATER THE WEATHER went sideways, turning unseasonably hot for Maine's last week in June – ninety-eight simmering, sweltering, clambake-steamy degrees. The mugginess shortened tempers, and nighttime brought negligible relief from the heat's onslaught.

At Eagles' Rest, within the stout walls, its occupants slept peacefully, drifting away to the hum of the air-conditioner's one-note song. In homes without that amenity, some folks made do with the mad-hornet drone of fans sweeping the air like radar. Others slept on screened-in porches, where no-see-ums snickered, sneaking in, uninhibited by the finest of mesh screens.

One person walked, wary, and watching.

Robert Morgan's big truck, black and sleek with chrome accents like jewelry on a paramour, was parked beside a low stonewall fence. Watcher climbed in the cab, lowered the window a scant inch, snapped the door locks, and settled back in the seat.

Shadows stretched into a seamless meld with the dark of night. Across the inky ballroom, the silvery moon waltzed with gossamer clouds. The eerie call of a loon, the haunting hoot of an owl, and the flutter of dusky wings blended with the soft whispering of pine trees. It seemed so peaceful.

Until Robert Morgan struck a discordant chord into the night's lullaby. An old car wheezed and coughed as it rumbled into the driveway.

He got out and slammed the car door. "Bye, Beeje. Thanks, ol' buddy." As usual, Billy Jones was marginally less tanked than his passenger.

Billy gunned the engine, creating a dark noxious cloud of exhaust as he backed out in an uneven course. He just missed hitting one of the pair of cedar trees that defined the front edge of the drive.

"Watch out for the fuzz," Bob hollered at the retreating car.

Bob shuffle-stepped up the slight incline of the driveway, skidding in the chunks of crushed rock that had been loosened by yesterday's rain. He steered an uneven course toward his truck.

The little cottage's porch light spilled its yellow beam from the cracked globe, slinking down the sagging, peeling white-painted porch steps. Its feeble effort cast faint illumination over the driveway.

Within the dark interior of the truck's cab, Watcher observed Bob's progress. The driver's side window was down a little bit so that Watcher heard every word of Bob's ranting monologue. The dark-tinted windows assured further anonymity.

"How dare her t' challenge me! She needs t' learn I'm the boss ..." Bob trailed off, looked around, and scratched his head.

"When was it? Yesterday? Day before? Ain't got no time clock to punch. Punch? Yeah, decking my boss tonight maybe wasn't too smart," he snickered. "But it was me that got kicked out of the Dipped Oar. Not him."

A tangled string of unimaginative cussing and slurred epithets swirled around his head as if the vapors of the very spirits he had chugged down were visible.

"She can't just leave," he mumbled. Bob put a shaky hand on his forehead. "Gawd, my head. Mebbe I oughta quit drinkin'."

Under the tree, one of the shadows moved.

"Huh? Who'zare?" Silence met his question. "Zat you, sugar?"

"Whoooo!" followed by swooshing wings was the answer.

Bob leaned against the sleek front fender and pulled a whiskey bottle from under his belt. He opened his mouth and tilted the bottle. Whiskey leaked down his chin. He wiped the slobber with the back of his grungy hand and belched.

As if slogging through the sluggish depths of soused logic, he continued the disjointed conversation with himself. "Truck … ain't driving it, not me. I've had too many b-bottles over the yardarm." Bob cocked his head to one side in a crooked parody of an owl, chuckled, then he hiccoughed. After a moment he said, "That's a'right. I'm waitin' for ya." Fumbling, he stowed the bottle back under his belt.

Bringing his his left arm close to his face, Bob mumbled, "Can't see. Dumb watch, never did work right."

Watcher was grateful for the invisibility behind tinted

26

windows, but wary of making any movement.

Bob picked his way along the side and around to the rear of the truck, holding onto the rear fender for balance.

The camper's door handle didn't budge. "Huh, locked. Got to keep little wifey out. Hehehe. Those undies under the cot sure aren't her Sunday granny whites, nuh-uh. What a kick, this one!"

Groping his way along the side of the truck, he passed by the driver's side door and hesitated. The doors were locked, but Watcher remained alert while Bob staggered toward the nose of the truck.

Using the stonewall fence for a step-up, Bob managed to climb up onto the wide hood of the truck without penalty to himself or the whiskey bottle stuffed under his belt. He settled down on his side, crossways of the hood with his back to the windshield, using one arm as a pillow for his head. With a piggish snort, he gave in to the arms of Morpheus.

4

Pattysue Morgan Is Safe

Wednesday, June 27th, morning

PATTYSUE SLUMPED ON THE COUCH in the cluttered living room, watching the Wednesday early-morning talk show without really seeing it.

Carrie bustled about the kitchen, busy cooking a big breakfast. Pattysue turned her attention away from the talking heads to watch her older sister, noticing that Carrie looked awfully tired this morning.

"Thank you for rescuing us," Pattysue said. "We couldn't have managed without you." Taking refuge at her sister's house in Willow Grove was her first thought last Saturday morning when she and Kaleen fled from her drunken husband.

"That's what family's for," Carrie said while running water in the sink. "Don't worry about anything. You're safe here." Carrie brushed her dishwater blonde curls behind her ears.

Happy squeals filtered in from the back yard where little Kaleen and her Unk Coop were playing toss and fetch. From past experience, Pattysue knew that four-year-old Kaleen was doing the tossing, and her uncle, the fetching.

"It's sure nice t' hear her laughing again." Pattysue's

words slurred. The pain medications made her words come out fuzzy. She shook her head and wished she hadn't done so. She had hoped to quit taking the meds tomorrow, but the way she felt right now, maybe not. "Coop is awfully good to take today off, special for her sake."

"Ayuh, she's a happy little tyke. She bounced right back. She sure loves her uncle, and he loves her." Carrie tossed her wad of gum into the trashcan under the sink and washed her hands. "Since he owns the accounting business, he can take time off when he wants to, except during tax season, of course."

Carrie flipped the pancakes with an expert toss, then slipped sizzling, fat bacon slices out of the big frying pan onto a paper towel-lined platter. She poured the grease into a tin can resting in the sink then set the frying pan on the back burner, ready for the second batch of bacon.

"Dang it! Got grease on my glasses." She washed them in the sink and dried them on a paper towel.

"Now, Pattysue, don't you worry 'bout nothing, Bob won't be coming for you here, either. Good for nothing b—" She paused before finishing the word and replaced her big green-framed glasses. "No looking back now. You need to move forward."

The persistent ringing of the phone interrupted their morning's peace.

Carrie hurried to the living room and checked the caller ID. She grimaced, lowered the TV volume with the remote, and picked up the handset.

Pattysue whispered, "Speakerphone."

Carrie pushed the speaker button. "Hello, Jobina," she

said to their cousin.

"How'd you know it was me? You got a black spy box, too?"

"What d'you want?" Carrie growled.

"You don't need to get snippy with me! They said Pattysue filed abuse charges on her husband. Did she call you? Is she there with you? I want to talk to her."

Pattysue shook her head. Jobina Court was the last person she wanted to talk to this morning, other than Bob.

"Yes, she's here. No, Jobina, you ain't gonna talk to her. She's resting. Pain meds, you know," she explained, walking back to the kitchen with Pattysue right behind her.

"Miracle meds, miracle cures. That's what they told me. I don't believe any of it."

"Believe what? What *are* you talking about?"

Pattysue was also curious about Jobina's story, in spite of her disinclination to talk to this odd duck in the family pond.

"Tsk, tsk, tsk."

"Does anyone really say 'tsk' anymore?" Carrie muttered.

"What'd you say?"

"Nothing." Carrie set the phone on the kitchen counter. She removed the cap from the maple syrup and placed the bottle in the microwave. The buttons beeped as she pushed the timer.

"W-what's that noise? Ohmigosh, you've got one, too!"

"One what?"

"Beeping! That's Morse code! I knew it, your phone's tapped!"

Before Carrie could answer, Jobina rushed onward. "Did

you know I was attacked? Yesterday! And no one gives a rat's hiney. They're the screwiest bunch of nitwits at that hospital. All my records have disappeared. 'Lost,' they said. Deliberately, I'll bet. One of the fruitloop nurses made me drink a diet soda – said it was good for me. Aspartame. Diet before dying. I know that stuff is poison and—"

"Did they give you anything else?" Carrie interrupted Jobina's tale of woe. "Like your regular pills?"

Pattysue clamped her hand across her mouth, stifling a snigger.

"They gave me a pill all right, a miracle drug. Guaranteed to cure death threats, they said, a pill to deflect bullets. *That* should really sell! Pills guaranteed to cure the delusion that I was attacked. But I've got bruises to prove it. They said so."

"Who said, Jobina?" Carrie shook her head as if shedding cobwebs.

"The Communicator always knows." Her voice increased in volume then trailed off.

"Shades of *The Shadow Knows*?" Pattysue whispered.

"What? What was that?"

"Nothing, Jobina." Carrie raised her voice as she moved toward the stove. "Really, you need help." She slid a handful of bacon slices into the hot frying pan.

"Help? They said I'm a spy. Me! I heard them talking in the hall about me after they made me take this miracle pill. That's no help. A bullet's not a delusion!"

Pattysue mouthed, "A bullet?"

Carrie nodded, rolling her eyes. "Have you taken your meds today, Jobina? You know which—"

31

"Witch? We got some in our family. Did you know that? Goes way back, Carrie. Great Aunt Harriet, jaybird, and … they drown witches. Women and men witches."

"Jobina, I really don't know what you're talking about. I gotta get back to cooking breakfast. Bye, Jobina."

"Carrie, you're rude. What about poor ol' Bob? No miracle drugs for Bob-Bob-Bobbing along … too late … he had a date …" she sang, her high-pitched, tuneless voice fading like a train running out of steam.

Carrie turned the bacon over, the slices crackling and popping in the hot grease. In the background, the quiet TV news had faded, giving way to a blaring commercial for a used-car dealership.

"Your line *is* bugged! I can hear it! Soon it will be all over. It's too late for…"

"Say good-bye, Jobina. I just did," Carrie interrupted. She returned the phone to its base in the living room.

The sound of frantic spattering and sizzling sent her hurrying back to the kitchen stove where Pattysue was rescuing the bacon before it was burnt to ashes.

While Carrie made more pancakes, Pattysue took a quick shower and dressed in comfortable clothes. A broken arm limited her fashion options. On her way back to the kitchen, she glanced at the small table by the front door. One of Kaleen's little hair bows was in the metal tray where they threw their keys and other minutia. She frowned at the jumble of keys, perplexed. Giving up, she put the bow in the pocket of her dress, walked to the kitchen, and sat down.

"That woman's pure poison," Carrie said, plunking her chubby body down on the seat across from her sister. "Her scrunched-up face looks like she was weaned on pickle juice. She's plum wonkered out. Leap-frogging topics, she doesn't string two sane thoughts together in one breath! Wicked shame. What does she do when she ain't blabbering nonsense?"

Carrie was letting off steam, so Pattysue didn't answer. She was following a rogue thought of her own that she couldn't quite pin down. She wanted to get better, get off this pain medication, and get her life back. No. Start her life *over*.

Pattysue recalled her visit to Baywater County Emergency Clinic. "At the Clinic, Dr. Grayson was so kind," she said. The young medic had held her hand and looked so earnest. He urged her to report the abuse and get out of the relationship. "He even said I'd be pretty again, after the bruises fade. No one has called me 'pretty' for a long time." She sighed and shrugged, wanting to believe it.

"You will be pretty again, Pattysue. It just takes time."

"I know, thanks." Changing the subject, Pattysue said, "Poor Cousin Jobina. Too bad."

"Too bad we're related, or Jobina's condition?" Carrie asked. "Hmm, forgot to make up orange juice. I don't know where my mind is this morning. We'll eat in a few minutes."

"Smells good. I'm hungry."

While her sister rummaged in the freezer for the orange juice concentrate, Pattysue elaborated. "I mean she has some really strange views on things. Like some of the stuff she said today. She's family, but I never liked her much, and neither did you."

She sat up straighter and patted her long French braid. "Thanks for braiding my hair, Carrie."

"You're welcome, Sis. These curls of mine are a curse."

"It looks cute when you fix it up. My hair would never do that."

"Ain't never satisfied, are we?"

Carrie dumped the orange juice concentrate into a big glass pitcher and added water. She punched the frozen slurry with a spoon as if she were pounding on her worst enemy.

"Do you remember what happened? Why Jobina's like this?" Pattysue shifted her position on the hard bench seat.

"She started to weird out right after her baby died. It's been, what, ten, twelve years, or so?" Carrie eased up on her onslaught of the juice.

"Wasn't it a crib death? That's what Dad said, I think. I was too young then to know much."

"That's what they said. Her husband died a year later. Boat accident. Word went around that maybe James didn't drown accidentally. I still don't believe it was an accident. Jay was a powerful swimmer, and that made folks wonder. Double whammy for Jobina – must have tipped her over the edge. Dad told me the police and the doctors walked it right to her both times. Don't think they were ever satisfied. No real evidence, so they dropped it. Lately she says she's being watched. Might not be a bad idea to watch her, come to think of it."

"Does she go out much? I don't remember seeing her around town." Pattysue moved the napkin holder out of the way. Carrie set down a platter heaped with pancakes.

"She drives some but sticks pretty close to home. She's usually not so vocal. Sounded worse this time, so something must have set her off. It ain't a full moon, so that can't be it."

Pattysue grinned. "Is she certifiable?"

"Nope, don't think so. Poisonous, but reasonably harmless. Well, if that ain't an oxymoron!" Carrie wondered aloud about what the real purpose had been for Jobina's phone call. From local gossip, maybe Jobina had heard something?

"I'd better check into that right after breakfast," she said. She opened the kitchen's back door and yelled, "Coop! Kaleen! C'mon, troops, let's eat!"

5

Pattysue Hears
News Red and Prose Purple

Wednesday, June 27th, mid-morning

BREAKFAST WAS FINISHED, although Pattysue hadn't eaten enough to justify her earlier claims of hunger. She was thumbing through a magazine, ignoring the mid-morning news.

An *Urgent Breaking News* alert flashed, catching her attention. Red letters trailed across the lower edge of the wide screen, overriding the middle-aged anchorman's blather with the young, very pretty meteorologist.

He turned to face the viewing audience out in TV land. "This news just in! We are going live action to Baysinger Cove in Baywater County, where TV-ZONE reporter Randy Lemoyne is standing by."

The visual shifted from the static newsroom to a familiar pastoral wooded scene.

"Carrie! Come see this. Quick, Carrie!"

Pattysue grabbed the remote and turned up the volume. Carrie, wiping her hands on a towel tucked into the waistband of her wrinkled shorts, joined her sister on the couch. An avalanche of magazines slid to the floor unheeded.

* * * * *

Randy Lemoyne wiped his sweaty face and shoved the limp red bandanna into his back pocket. He listened for the cameraman to start the countdown. He rearranged his face to reflect "solemn." He straightened up, standing tall, in serious studied profile to the camera.

"Three. Two. One. Live!"

Randy turned toward the camera. With a deep sigh he placed his right hand over his heart. In funereal tones, he said, "The Baywater County Sheriff is investigating the unfortunate discovery of a body found at a private residence in Baysinger Cove, which might," he paused for effect, "or might not," he hesitated again, "have been an accident."

He bowed his head a bit, striking a reverent attitude, to allow the weight of his profound words to carry out to his viewers out in TV land.

* * * * *

In one living room, a retired English teacher was shaking her finger at the screen. With a sardonic laugh, she scolded the oblivious reporter. "Unfortunate for whom? The *discovery* was an accident? You grammar-less moron! I taught you better than that."

In another living room, a fat-faced man rubbed the day-old stubble on his bruised cheek. Recognizing the house in the background, he said, "Gotcha, ya mangy old cur," adding a long list of other derogatory curses.

Jimmy Howe said, "Yessiree, Bob, ya finally got what was comin' to ya, ya wife stealer."

The barman at the Dipped Oar regretted the loss of a good customer and yesterday's unpaid bar tab.

The killer was satisfied that the payback plan had worked.

* * * * *

Pattysue and Carrie were perched on the edge of the couch, staring at the unfolding news story in big screen brilliance.

In the background behind Randy Lemoyne, people milled about in morbid curiosity, watching a body bag strapped on a stretcher being loaded into a waiting ambulance.

"That looks like Jobina!"

Pattysue leaned forward. "Where?"

"There, walking behind that dipstick reporter."

"You mean the woman wearing a kerchief?"

Carrie replied, "It sure looks like her. But what's she doing there?"

* * * * *

The on-site camera switched from Randy to background "atmosphere" then panned to Sheriff Walker Bainbridge. Randy introduced him to the viewers with a flourish.

Frowning against the glare of the sun reflecting off the camera lens, the sheriff said, "About an hour ago, a jogger running on Bookman Road discovered the body of an adult male. Pending notification of relatives, there will be no other information released at this time." He turned on his boot heels, walked away from the camera, and headed toward the ambulance.

The camera swiveled back to the star reporter. "Live news from TV-ZONE, where it's 'Z One' place to hear all the news that is news. We're here in the cozy little hamlet of Baysinger Cove. Sheriff Walker Bainbridge has just given us a brief statement."

Randy continued reporting in his best theatrical manner, unaware of uncensored editorial comments off-site. "We are gazing at a busy little village where the majority of the residents live year-round, peppered with many sweet summer cottages. Like a necklace adorning Serenadelle Lake, the idyllic tranquility of this timeless hamlet, by this poisonous weed, has forever scarred the pristine landscape."

Striking a somber attitude, he turned his best side once again in profile to the camera. "This is roving reporter Randy Lemoyne for TV-ZONE." After a short pause, he snapped his head over his right shoulder and stared straight at the camera. "Back to you, Jack."

* * * * *

The English teacher groaned and snapped off her TV. "Miserably misplaced modifiers, purple prose, and spurious stage works! I am sorely tempted to write a letter to Randy's boss."

The fat man said, "Longfellow, he ain't."

* * * * *

Pattysue sprang from the couch, the news having jolted

her out of her lethargic haze. "That road. That's my driveway! His truck. Oh, no! What if it's Bob?" She remembered her fury-induced statement at the Clinic: "He just wants murdering."

Carrie sat on the couch, arms crossed, tapping her fist against her mouth.

Pattysue flittered around, unable to settle. "Oh, Carrie, what if it's Bob?" she repeated.

Dropping her hand, Carrie replied, "What if it is? It ain't like he didn't have it coming."

Surprised at the venom in her sister's voice, Pattysue stared at her. Carrie yawned.

Pattysue resumed pacing around the living room, tossing newspapers, burrowing through magazines, moving stacks of junk mail. "Where's your phone book, Carrie?"

Carrie pulled it out from behind the couch cushion and handed it to her. "Who're you wanting to call?"

"The sheriff. I've got to know!"

Shaking like an aspen leaf in the breeze, hampered by the use of only one hand, she rustled the thin pages of the phone book. She recalled sitting in the doctor's office at the Clinic, talking to the sheriff. He had given her a card that she tucked in her purse. She dropped the phone book, hurried to the spare bedroom, dumped her purse out on the bed, and unearthed the business card. Returning to the living room, Pattysue punched in the number.

"Sheriff Bainbridge's office. How may I help you?" inquired a pleasant female voice.

Carrie stood up and walked to the kitchen.

"I want to speak to the sheriff. P-please."

Carrie watered the spindly, nearly-dead-by-drowning ivy teetering on the near edge of the windowsill. She pushed it back on the sill before it fell into the sink.

"May I give him a message? Hang on, he just walked in."

To the bass voice who came on the line, Pattysue said, "Uh, I'm … I just saw the news. The man on Bookman Road … I think that he … he may be … my husband, B-Bob. Robert Morgan."

"Where are you right now?"

"M-my sister's. In Willow Grove." She recited the address.

"Please stay there, Mrs. Morgan. I will be along shortly to see you."

Clicking the phone off, Pattysue stared at the impersonal clutter on the coffee table. "Of course I'm here at Carrie's. I've got no other place to go. Home? It's safe now. Now that Bob is dead. Dead!"

She burst into tears, wondering aloud about what she was going to do, how she could take care of herself and Kaleen both on her pitifully small salary from working part-time at the bookstore. "Maybe Harold will let me work full-time when Kaleen goes to school in the fall."

"Would Mrs. Sanger watch her for you, if you go on full-time?" Carrie handed her sister a box of tissues.

"I can ask her. She's right next door, and Kaleen loves her." Pattysue snuffled into the tissue.

"Anyway, you're better off without him. He's gone for good now." Carrie wrapped mother-comfort arms around her baby sister.

"What … what am I going to do? I don't have any

41

money. I can't work for a while at least."

"Don't worry. Coop and me, we'll take care of you."

Strident tones pierced the widow's sobs. Carrie grabbed the phone without looking at the screen. She clicked on the speaker, and set the phone down on the cluttered coffee table.

"You see the news?" the caller asked.

"What do you want now, Jobina?"

"Told you!" Jobina sang. "No smoke without fire."

"Oh, by the old lord Harry, just leave it alone."

"Where was *she* last night? Where were *you*? Out of sight, out of mind, out of luck. Yessiree Bobby! Outta luck! No magic pill for poor ol' Bobby."

Interrupting Jobina's harangue, Carrie said, "Good-bye, Jobina."

"You're mean! You should be nice to me. We're cousins."

"I said good-bye, Jobina." She clicked off the phone, staring at it like she didn't know what to do with it.

Pattysue said, "That woman gets crazier every minute."

"She's way over the plumb bob line. Wonder what she meant by …" Carrie trailed off. "No smoke without fire? What fire?"

6

Maggie Hears the News

Thursday, June 28ᵗʰ, early morning

MAGGIE HAD JUST STEPPED OFF the staircase when she met Larkin coming from the master bedroom. "Good morning," she said to her aunt.

"And a lovely good morning to you, my dear," Larkin replied after their hug.

In the breakfast room, Larkin greeted her husband with a kiss.

Rod poured coffee for them both. "You just missed Walker," he said. "Our sheriff had some bittersweet news."

"Oh, what was that?" Larkin took an exploratory sip of the steaming brew.

"Seems that scoundrel Bob Morgan died sometime late Tuesday or early Wednesday." He topped off his own cup.

On the table in front of him was today's New York Times crossword puzzle, which he worked in ink. Maggie was impressed since she rarely finished one of their complex puzzles, and she used a pencil.

"Mercy! It's always sad to hear of anyone dying so young. It is a mixed blessing for poor Pattysue, though," Larkin said. "Did he say anything more?"

"He didn't have much news, and won't have until the

M.E. report comes back. Say, Larkin, what's an eleven letter word for 'rebellious'? Begins with 'con' and the sixth letter is 'm'."

Larkin thought for a moment. Try 'contumacious,' darling."

"Ayuh, that's it. Thanks, m'love."

"Morgan?" Maggie took another sip of the welcome first cup of coffee.

"Yes, remember? You met Pattysue at the Sawmill the day you arrived," Larkin replied. "Bob was her husband."

"Oh, right. I guess all's well that ends well."

"Maggie!" Larkin scolded. She passed the butter dish to Maggie.

"Well, he was a blight on her life," Maggie answered before taking a bite of a fresh blueberry muffin.

"True, but still …"

7

Maggie Meets Baby and Friends

Saturday, June 30ᵗʰ, morning

SATURDAY MORNING REVEALED Mother Nature's benevolent face. The sun was shining with nary a cloud in the sky to spoil the day.

"Now, who'd you say this shower is for?" Maggie held her finger on the frilly pink ribbon's knot while Larkin tied the bow.

Larkin was making her usual creative magic happen with the wrapping and ribbons on this sweet package. The paper was awash with tiny pink umbrellas and bows. She had tied matching novelty buttons on ribbon streamers, gathering them together to make a fancy-dangle bow.

"Thank you, dear, you can let go now."

"It sure is a pretty quilt, all pink and pixies." Maggie said, extracting her finger from the knot. "And you're positive it's a girl?"

"The shower is for Kendra and Darren Parkwood," Larkin said. She tweaked the bow and fluffed the ribbons, tilting her head this way and that way to assure the bow's symmetry. "They wanted to wait until after the baby was born. Yes, *her* name is Jaden. We'll get to see the little cutie, too."

Glancing up at the clock, Maggie said, "It's just gone ten. What time is this shower?"

"Ten-thirty. The church is all of a five-minute drive. If we head over there now we might still find a good parking place."

Larkin snagged a parking slot one row back in the spacious, fast-filling parking lot. Maggie carried the bow-bedecked gift while they made slow progress into the fellowship hall. Larkin said hello to, or was greeted by, everyone she met.

Typical small town, Maggie mused. *I do believe that she does know everyone.*

Like a pro, Larkin wove through the chatter of women milling around the room. They found several seats together at the far end of the wide half-circle of chairs. Larkin took the package from Maggie. "I'll take this over to the gift table and get us some punch on the way back."

"I'll save your seat." Maggie set her purse in the empty chair beside her.

Pattysue's cast jogged Maggie's memory as to who she was. She was a bit surprised to see her here, a widow of a few days' duration. Pattysue was standing a short distance away. Beside her was a woman about the same height, but there the similarity ended.

She listed starboard toward plump, with very curly, dirty-blonde hair. Her square face, devoid of makeup, was peppered with a bumper crop of freckles. The woman wore large glasses, the frames a chartreuse color that, to Maggie's creative view, was frog underbelly green, which made the woman look like a nearsighted, brown-eyed amphibian. The grass-green tee shirt completed the illusion and did little to hide the abundance of what it covered. Her straight-from-the-dryer brown shorts and chunky-tire sandals made Maggie, who was wearing a nice cotton blouse and black dress jeans, feel overdressed.

Pattysue turned and asked, "You're staying with the Richardsons, right?"

Maggie stood up. "Yes, I'm Maggie Storm Blue. Rod and Larkin Richardson are my uncle and aunt." She paused and leaned forward. "May I extend my sympathies to you?"

Pattysue took the proffered tissue from her companion and wiped her nose. "It's all right." She sat down, leaving an empty chair between herself and Maggie.

Maggie regained her seat and changed the subject. "That's a very pretty necklace you're wearing."

"Thank you." Pattysue brightened as she fingered the lustrous pearl suspended from a fine gold chain. "Papa gave it to me last Christmas. My sister's got one too. I never take mine off." She turned to her companion. "Where's yours, Carrie?"

Carrie's hand flew to her neck. "Uh, I ... "

"Oh, I'm forgetting my manners. This is Carrie Larradeau, my sister."

These two look no more like sisters than a cat and dog, Maggie thought uncharitably.

Pattysue's pale auburn hair was French-braided. She wore a light apricot, gauzy summer dress and dainty white sandals, an outfit that suited her delicate frame. A copious application of makeup made a brave job in covering the bruise around her eye, evidence that she had a sense of pride

47

in her personal appearance, in spite of her current physical appearance.

A woman dropped down in the empty seat, interrupting Maggie's inspection of Pattysue.

"Is it? I don't believe it! Maggie Storm Blue, it's really you?"

"Ye-es." She riffled through pages of memory, going back … "Autumn Skye Taylor!"

"Yes! Remember in school how we used to roll our eyes at the affectation of our names?" Autumn clutched Maggie's hand in both of hers.

"Oh, quite. We couldn't fathom how our mothers came up with them!" Maggie laughed and placed her free hand atop Autumn's.

"You know it! We had lots of giggle time over it, though," Autumn agreed. "Did you ever marry again?"

"No. How about you?"

"I'm still married to Chad Taylor. Thirty-five years, if you can believe that."

"Oh, what fun it is to see you again!"

In high school, eons ago, they had been each other's Number One Best Friend. They had kept in touch after graduation through infrequent letters and phone calls, then e-mail, but long distances discouraged many visits.

"The last time I saw you, neither one of us had gray hair!" Maggie exclaimed.

* * * * *

Maggie's grandparents were in their late seventies when she last lived with them in the old farmhouse in North

Belgrade, near Great Pond. Grandfather had reached the age where he was no longer physically able to clear the driveway of snow. Relocating to Hallowell assured that teenaged Maggie would not miss an undue amount of school.

She was a very reluctant transfer student. Her first day in the new school was, to her, comparable to having a cavity filled without the benefit of Novocain. The first hour was sophomore English class. A slender, tall, red-haired girl turned around in her chair and faced Maggie. Bright-eyed with a cheek-wrinkling grin, she said, "I'm Autumn Skye Miller. Who are you?"

Maggie had grasped the lifeline and smiled right back.

From that moment, they forged a friendship that had borne the distance, both of mileage and time. One or the other would drop out for a season. But when the two friends picked up again, it was as though no time had passed between Then and Now. This recent gap was over twenty years wide.

* * * * *

Larkin handed Maggie a dripping plastic cup of something fizzy pink. "Of course, pink for the baby girl. I do wonder what they would have concocted for a boy." She sat down in the chair Maggie had saved for her.

Maggie took an exploratory sip. "It's cranberry juice and ginger ale. Tasty." She set her cup under her chair and stood up.

"Aunt Larkin, you'll never guess who this is!" She introduced the two women.

Larkin returned Autumn's pleasant smile. "I'm very

pleased to meet you, Autumn. I hope you two will have some time to spend together while Maggie's here. She's staying with us, of course. You are coming to the Shindig on the Fourth, aren't you? Since you're old friends, it will be especially nice for Maggie to have you there."

"Thank you, Mrs. Richardson. The whole town's buzzing about it. Mom and Dad will be there. We will be, too. Thank you. We wouldn't miss it now." When Autumn mentioned her parents' names, Larkin recognized them.

"Sorry, but the weekend following the Fourth, Chad and I are leaving for a long overdue vacation. We are driving across the lower states to California, and then we'll head up the Pacific coastline. We'll stop in Seattle where we'll spend some time with our middle daughter. Our plan is to return via the northern route."

"I'm sorry, too, but we'll keep—"

An insistent loud clapping interrupted their eager-to-get-reacquainted chatter. Maggie regained her seat in a hurry. The attention-demander was a gray-haired, short, pear-shaped woman wearing a salmon pink blouse and skin-tight navy blue slacks. She swaggered to the front of the wide crescent-shaped group of chairs.

Autumn leaned over and whispered to Maggie. "Some women shouldn't wear slacks."

"Or pink," Maggie replied, stifling a snicker.

Mrs. Pink Blouse glared at them. She clapped her hands again, and the room quieted down.

"OKAY, everyone, let's get this party started!" she shouted. "We have the Proud Parents, Darren and Kendra Parkwood, here with our Brand New Guest of Honor!" she declared. She waved her hands, in a manner suggestive of announcing the newest Miss Universe, in the direction of an embarrassed young couple. They sat fidgeting on hard metal folding chairs situated between the two over-burdened gift tables.

"Please welcome them and my First Great-Grandchild, Miss Jaden Laura Audrey Fredericka Parkwood!"

Drum roll presumed.

The new mother stood, blushing all the way to her magenta hairline, and held up the sleeping baby for everyone to see.

The applause died down. Larkin leaned over to Maggie, her hand shielding her mouth. "That's Audrey Fremantle. Her daughter, Fredericka Larkspur, bought that Tri-A house. Freddi is Kendra's mama. Darren's mama, Laura, is talking to Kendra now."

Audrey bobbled toward them. Her wide, synthetic smile revealed a slight gap between her upper front teeth. "We'll go round the circle. Introduce yourself and guests. We'll start right here!" she bubbled, placing her stubby hand on Maggie's shoulder. "You first, Larkin."

After the introductions, silly games followed, an effective icebreaker that got everyone laughing. Then came the opening of presents and more presents, punch and cookies, and talk and gossip.

At first, Birdie Mandrill was seated at the midpoint of the half-circle of chairs, but she never stayed perched for long. She hopped from one person to another, just like her feathery namesake, gathering gossip in the manner of plucking worms for a savory lunch.

Larkin pointed Birdie out to Maggie. "She's Baysinger Cove's own personal gossipmonger. The root of news-vine begins with her. Don't tell her anything unless you want it broadcasted all over town. By the way, my hairdresser, Peggy, told me that Robert Morgan's funeral is Monday."

Three hours later they were in Larkin's car. She turned left onto Camp Road while Maggie fanned herself with a limp thank-you card.

"I simply cannot believe the deplorable manners of some people," Larkin declared, her drawl expanding the syllables, emphasizing her disgust. "The *very* idea! Audrey handing out computer generated, generic thank-you cards as we left. How crass is that?"

"At least Kendra loved the quilt and didn't just call it a blanket."

"Her grandmother is a quilter, so Kendra knows better. Otherwise, I would have given her a gift certificate."

Larkin turned the A/C fan on high. "You're a trooper to come with me today."

"No bother at all. After the first few people, I was wandering in the name jungle. It sure was fun to see Autumn again. Small world, this small town."

"Everywhere is small anymore with the Internet and television bringing everything worldwide into the immediate. And Birdie to help it along on the local level."

"I'm surprised you heard of Morgan's funeral from someone other than Birdie, if she's so gossipy."

"Birdie doesn't call me," Larkin said without rancor.

Maggie glanced at her aunt. "Whyever not?"

"Because, when I hear news or gossip, I never tell Birdie

anything. Morgan's funeral is at one o'clock Monday afternoon at the Baptist Church in Augusta. We're going because Pattysue's grandmother is a friend of mine. Do you want to go, or stay home?"

In books, the murderer attends the victim's funeral. A chance for me to sleuth, maybe! "Oh, I'll go with you, I guess."

As Larkin slowed for the traffic light, Maggie asked, "Weren't you surprised to see Pattysue at the shower?"

"She and Kendra were classmates. Carrie probably thought it would do her good to get out and socialize for a little bit."

When the eastbound traffic was clear, Larkin turned right onto Morrilton Road. She pulled left into the parking lot of The Mercantile a few minutes later. "I need to get chocolate chips and cream cheese for raspberry truffle brownies. We'll have a scratch dinner tonight. Whatever's in the fridge that's a Must-Go must go."

"Sounds good to me. I'll help with the brownies if you want me to."

"To lick the beaters?" Larkin teased.

8

Maggie Considers Angels and Fools

Monday, July 2ⁿᵈ, early afternoon

"**AND MAY GOD HAVE MERCY** on his soul."

The minister snapped his Bible closed, the sound like a gunshot shattering the total silence. He glanced over at the casket.

"Robert Brock Morgan has passed on. The members of his family are left to carry on without him." He paused, laid the Bible down on the pulpit then stepped out from behind the pulpit. "Comfort them as they mourn the loss of husband, father, son, grandson, and nephew."

The earlier squall had caused the outside temperature to drop by a few degrees but had done nothing to alleviate the claustrophobic mugginess seeping into the old, crowded church. Maggie was sitting between her family and her friends on a solid oak pew. Larkin and Rod were on her right, with Autumn and Chad sitting on her left. The memorial card she was using for a fan was ineffectual at best.

"Did he really have this many friends, or are they making sure he's really gone?" Maggie whispered to her uncle.

Walking the solemn processional past the plain metal casket, Pattysue passed by without stopping, staring straight ahead. Cooper Larradeau had his arm around her shoulders. Carrie peered into the casket for a long moment as if seeking reassurance that Bob Morgan was really there before hurrying after her husband and sister. Two gray-haired and four white-haired couples followed. The parents and grandparents, Maggie suspected. They stopped for a long final look before moving toward the side door.

Row by row, people moved one at a time down the center aisle, behind the family.

Maggie scanned the crowd, wondering if the murderer was here. *As if I'd know him if he was,* she chided herself. At the back of the church she saw a tall, tough-looking man talking to a short, middle-aged man who was the size of a youth. The small man waved his left hand. The sun threw rainbows from his full-caret pinkie ring. Only one man she knew would ever wear such ostentatious jewelry.

Victor! What's he doing here? What I know about my slimy cousin doesn't jive with what little I know about Robert Morgan. Maybe I need to find out more about the recently deceased, beyond his being a drunk and a wife batterer.

Now standing outside in the steamy sunshine, Maggie basked like a cat, savoring the warmth of the sun, and grateful for the light breeze.

Rod said to the little group assembled on the lawn, "Larkin and I have some things to do this afternoon. Maggie, would you mind riding back with Chad and Autumn, if that's not an imposition, Chad?"

Chad assured him that it was no bother, and Maggie was just as eager to renew the friendship with her old classmates. She wondered what her relatives were up to today. Probably gathering more stuff for the Shindig that would be happening two days from now.

Autumn nudged Maggie. "Come on, let's get out of here. Chad wants to eat at the Sawmill. I don't know about you, but I'm hungry."

They started down the stone-paved path to the parking lot, chatting nineteen to the dozen. Maggie noticed two big men standing a short way off to their right. Before she could ask Chad about them, a man inserted himself directly in front of her, causing her to halt short. She stiffened, shifted her balance, and brought her fists up to her waist.

"Remember me, Mags?" the man challenged in a singsong voice.

Chad reached for his cell phone. Maggie stopped him with an imperceptible shake of her head.

She assessed this boorish interloper, her stare colder than the stone on which she stood.

"Victor *Vincent* Turner, *the* Second," he said as he looked her down and up. Way up. "You haven't really forgotten me, have you, Mags?" he asked.

"No, I haven't, more's the pity." Her nose wrinkled like she'd just stepped in a still-steaming cow pie. *Ew-yuck!*

He wore a top-designer, tailored suit, and a French-cuffed lavender shirt with pearl cuff links. One was missing a pearl. The diamond stickpin in his elegant silk tie flashed fire in the sunlight. Thick glass in thin gold frames rested on the bridge of his buzzard beak nose. For his size and stature, he took after his mother. June was a petite woman with delicate features, who was anything but sweet natured. His attitudes and mindset were all hers as well: devious and mean.

Vincent stuck out his hand. With misgivings, Maggie shook it.

Following his limp-wrist, clammy handshake, she had an overwhelming urge to wipe her hand on her skirt.

"What do you want?" she demanded, contrary to her early years of be-a-lady training that struggled in vain to surface.

"You're getting yourself wedged tight into Uncle Rod's good graces these days, I hear. Living in the lap of luxury, Mags? Looking out for the main prize, hmm?" he taunted.

Maggie took a deep breath and looked down. Wearing heels, she towered over Victor by a full eight inches. She bent forward, invading Victor's personal space. In a low, clear voice, she bit off the words. "Hear me well. Mister. Victor. Vincent. Turner. *The.* Second. My Christian name is Maggie. Got it?" She poked his tie with a sharp fingernail. "It is by the grace of God alone that I have not slapped that sneer off your smug face." Poke.

If God takes care of fools and angels, she thought, *there's little danger of me sprouting wings anytime soon.*

"However, I do not want your jealous green slime on my hands. It is *no* business of yours," she sing-songed his hated nickname, "Little Vicky." Poke.

Maggie's friends and family had learned early on that when her jade-green eyes shifted to the dark green color of malachite, and her voice dropped to a lower register, her quicksilver temper was ridin' high, which guaranteed that a razor-sharp tongue-lashing was imminent. Though an easy-going and kind temperament, fools she suffered not at all, gladly or otherwise. She stepped a bit closer to the immediate object of her ire. An image of her guardian angels lining up for hazardous-duty pay flitted across her mind.

"What I am, or am not, doing is *my* business. Not yours. Got it?" She poked his chest again, a bit harder. The repeated pokes put major dents in his posh name-brand tie.

"You are not welcome in my world." Maggie closed the space between them. Poke.

Victor stumbled when he backed up again and tripped over a rock. The dramatic effect of his arrogant bantam rooster stance was lost with his ignoble retreat from Maggie's repeated jabs.

A tall, stocky, tough-looking man, the one who had been talking with Victor in the church, was standing a few feet away. He had a very amused look on his scarred face.

In a voice edged with ice, she said, "You're in our way, *mister*."

Her temper at war with her upbringing and faith, she struggled against carrying out her earlier threat to slap him. "Move. Now."

Startled, Victor stepped aside, "Uh-oh, little orphan Maggie's got claws!" Victor turned and headed with less dignity and more alacrity than an easy-come-easy-go manner in the opposite direction. His buddy loped along beside him.

Chad Taylor slipped his cell phone back in his pocket. He took Maggie's right elbow and Autumn locked Maggie's left arm in hers as they walked to the parking lot. They passed the two big men. Chad waved in their direction.

"Those two men standing over there? The one on the left is our county sheriff, Walker Bainbridge," Chad said. "If things had gotten out of hand, Maggie, they had your back."

Before Maggie could ask Chad about the identity of the second man, Autumn said, "Maggie, who was that smarmy guy?"

"You don't know him?"

"Nuh-uh."

"Not missing much. Surprised me big time, he did. Friends, I apologize for my hissy-fit back there."

"Don't worry about that," Chad replied. "You were holding your own, without any help from us. I almost called the police until I saw the sheriff. He watched the whole thing."

Chad unlocked the car and held the doors open, first for Autumn, then Maggie.

"He sure seemed to know you," Autumn said as she buckled her seat belt.

"He does, unfortunately. One of my shirttail cousins, Victor's about five years older than me. Uncle Rod's sister, June, is Victor's mother. He's an only child and a wicked spoiled brat. Evidently he has refined the brat act over time. He looks like a silk purse, but he's really the sow's *rear*."

"You shouldn't malign the poor pig." Autumn turned and gave Maggie a sideways grin.

"As kids, we butted heads a lot. Talk about mixed metaphors!" Maggie laughed, her earlier outburst forgotten. "Don't care if he is related. I cannot stand him, never have, and never will. Ain't Christian, but there you have it. Never said I was perfect, just forgiven."

"If he missed your point, Maggie, he's as dense as those glasses he wears," Chad said. "Um, did you notice he was carrying a gun?" He stopped for a traffic light.

"Yes, I did. I went into journalistic mode to cope with the intrusion and took detailed inventory. Occupational hazard, that. Yeowser! That scene could have turned right ugly," she said, shuddering. "Why would he need a gun? This is Maine. 'Life in the Slow Lane' for pity's sake." Maggie quoted a Maine tourism campaign's slogan from earlier years.

"Could've. Too many witnesses maybe," Chad joked. He made the turn heading toward Baysinger Cove. "Even here, unfortunately, we have the criminal element."

Autumn brightened. "Oh, you bit his head off good and proper. I'd forgotten your temper!"

"Ye-es, but it's usually tamped down. I'm pretty even-keeled most of the time, but I never know when I'm going to tilt starboard. I was so steamed I barely registered anything Victor said. So, let's dismiss this for the worthless encounter that it was and go on to pleasanter subjects." Maggie began digging around in her purse for a lipstick.

"I'm all for that." Autumn was also rummaging for a lipstick in her spacious designer purse.

Maggie looked out the window. "This has changed so. I'd be so everwhichaways if I were driving."

"We've lived here all our lives, so we're used to the changes." Chad turned left into the Sawmill's parking lot. "Here we are, ladies, a good subject we all agree on. Let's go eat!"

9

Maggie Enjoys Food, Faith, and Friendship

Monday, July 2nd, mid-afternoon

"Why so sober, friend?" Maggie laid her fork across her plate. "You've not said much since we sat down, Autumn."

The little bell on the front door added a happy note to the chatter of people flocking into the Sawmill Hill Cafe that afternoon.

"I've been thinking about Bob Morgan's funeral. That was a real bring-downer," Autumn said, the corners of her mouth in a downward slope. "It was when he asked God to have mercy on Bob's soul, *that* gave me chills," she elaborated, folding a straw wrapper concertina fashion. "Seems like certain preachers always have to say that. It's too melodramatic for me. By the time the funeral comes around, it's too late anyway. The soul already went on to its destination at the moment of death."

Chad rested his arm across the seat back and hugged his wife. "Most funerals *are* depressing, honey."

Turning his attention back to Maggie, he said, "Bob went to church with his folks when he was a kid. Quit going in his late teens when he discovered easy booze and easy women."

"Did you and Bob hang out together any when you were

kids?" Maggie asked.

"Not socially. We both worked at the marina during school vacations. He was a little wild, a typical teenage male. Likeable, almost charismatic if he wanted to be, when he was sober."

Remembering the particulars of the obituary, Maggie asked, "Why was the funeral in Augusta?" She drained her glass of iced tea.

"The Morgan family is originally from Augusta. His grandparents still live there, but his parents live in Camden."

"Any other family?"

"No, he's an only child. His mother spoiled him. He could do nothing wrong, in her eyes. If he got into scrapes, his father would smooth it over. Whatever he wanted, he got − fast car, slick boat, hot women, and cold beer."

Heather refilled their drinks. "Anything else? No?" She removed the three empty plates and returned to the kitchen.

Autumn jabbed the straw between the ice cubes in her cream soda. "Pattysue was too good for him. We've been friends with her grandparents for years. That's why we went to the funeral today."

"Whyever did they marry? Well, that's a silly question. There's no accounting for where Cupid's arrow flies," Maggie said.

"True," Autumn agreed. "When she first started dating him I didn't think he was her type. Sometimes I think love's either blind or stupid. But Pattysue found herself pregnant. 'Doing the right thing,' Bob insisted on marrying her. She thought she didn't have much choice."

Maggie picked up the damp cocktail napkin and wiped

the condensation from the side of her iced tea glass. She balled up the soggy mess and left it on the table. "Where does Pattysue live?"

Chad replied, "She lives over on Bookman Road. It's an all-season, sturdy craftsman-style cottage."

Autumn said, "That reminds me about what Pastor Blessington told us on Sunday about choices."

Chad tapped his forehead. "Yeah, the pastor quoted Blaise Pascal. Shoot, I can't remember it verbatim. Anyway, Pascal was a French mathematician and philosopher back in the seventeenth century. Smart guy. I'll just have to wing it: 'I'd rather live believing that God is real, and die discovering He isn't, than to believe there *isn't* a God, and discovering, way too late, there *is* a God.' His sermon was all about choices."

Maggie drank the rest of her iced raspberry tea. "I believe what the Bible says. That's good enough for me."

"Don't you want to see the dessert menu? We've added some new items," Heather announced. "Or, how 'bout our Famous Double Fudge Pie? Tempt you, maybe?"

"Chocolate?" the trio asked in unison.

"Bring it on!" Chad ordered.

Several happy minutes later, wiping the dregs of chocolate from their lips, the trio settled back in their seats.

Maggie laid her fork across her plate. "Just how many years *has* it been?"

"We don't count the years, Maggie," Autumn answered, the kindness of her smile reaching her eyes. "Time makes no difference with a friendship like ours. How long since we last talked on the phone? More years than we need to think about. But you are *here* right now. We'll pick up right where we left off."

"As usual?"

"As usual."

"I promise, my friend, never to go so long between calls in the future."

"That promise goes both ways, Maggie." Autumn reached across the table and squeezed Maggie's hand.

"This may be too obvious," Chad interjected, "but could the distance factor have anything to do with not having current phone numbers for either parties?"

"Oh, quite," Maggie answered. "I moved a dozen times …"

"And we went to cell phones, ditching the landlines several years ago," Autumn said.

"Well, there you have it," Chad said. He stood and reached for his wife's hand.

10

Maggie Reminisces

Tuesday, July 3rd, mid-morning

MAGGIE AND LARKIN WERE UPSTAIRS in the spacious North Room. It overshadowed the kitchen, breakfast and dining areas, encompassing nearly one-third of the house's footprint. Larkin used it for her craft and quilting activities. The generous space accommodated the ladies who came for Quilt Circle sewing days, with room to spare.

The many storage areas included built-in drawers and shelves on all walls that weren't taken up by windows. Contents of the dozens of glass-fronted drawers were identified with small brass label holders. Along the wall against the stairwell to the garage was a bookcase holding Larkin's well-stocked library of needlework and craft books.

In yesterday's mail, Larkin had received two nice books on crazy quilt embroidery stitches. "Since there's nothing left to do for the Shindig until tomorrow morning, we can have a look at my new books," she said, passing one to Maggie.

It was Joan Waldman's *Quilt Savvy Embroidery Stitches*. After a few minutes, Maggie commented on it, "I like this one. Spiral bound, a nice format, and small enough to toss in a tote bag. There are so many wonderful variations of stitches here. I'll order one for myself when I get home."

Siam brought a scrap of ribbon over and dropped it on the floor at Maggie's feet. She picked it up and jiggled it in his face. He was batting away with wild abandon when an errant scrap of paper caught in the light breeze of the ceiling fan distracted him. Siam chased it over to a corner, then abruptly sat on his haunches and licked his pussy-willow toes. Maggie tossed the much-bedraggled ribbon into the wastebasket.

"I'm ready for some tea, aren't you?" Larkin asked.

Larkin and Maggie started down the stairs. Siam made a mad dash between them.

"He shudenoughta do that! It scares me every time, the little daredevil. I'm sure glad he has nine lives," Larkin exclaimed, grabbing for the handrail.

The daredevil made a beeline for the utility room. Sheba was right on the tail of the speeding cat. The dog's fur stood on end, a growl emanating from deep within the far reaches of her voice box, squaring off with the hissing bundle of feline arrogance now regally perched in her food dish.

"Sheba, stop! Siam, move over, you silly cat. They are such children!"

Larkin picked Siam up out of the disputed dish and plunked him down without ceremony well away from the dog. Sheba dropped to the floor intent on guarding her precious possession. She kept the dish snug between her front paws with her furry chin resting on the rim.

"That little scene means Siam's food dish is empty. Please get some kibble, Maggie, it's in the cabinet beside the sink. His bowl has to be on top of the old icebox or Sheba will eat his food, the big piggy. Siam won't touch Sheba's food but dearly loves to tease her."

Siam was making figure eights around Maggie's legs, talking up a blue streak while she scooped out kibble. He sailed up onto the icebox, his nose in the bowl before Maggie could put it down.

Larkin filled the dog's dish, stowed the dog food under the cabinet, and held the door open for Maggie to replace the bag of cat food. "It has a spring latch so Siam can't get the door open," she explained. "He's awfully clever."

"Why did you decide to build here?"

They walked to the kitchen and Larkin turned to face her. "When your grandparents died, you remember that the old farmhouse in North Belgrade became ours. Well, living year-round several miles in on a one-lane dirt road, and no neighbors within shouting distance, was unrealistic for people our ages. We stayed there while this house was being built, however. We had purchased this property about forty years ago. We paid practically nothing for it then compared to today's prices for waterfront acreage."

"I've been looking at some of the listings." Maggie watched her aunt's eyebrows shoot up. "Just curious! A tar-paper shack with a squinty glimpse of water on the far horizon is over the top, price-wise." She picked the newspaper out of the basket in the Lake Room and returned to the snack bar end of the kitchen island. "So, to have ten acres, with water on three sides, this place must be a worth a king's ransom."

Larkin laughed and joined her niece at the snack bar. "Very accurate assessment, my dear. We always intended to build here someday. Relentlessly, 'someday' came. We hired a local architect who had the talent to translate dreams into floor plans and elevations. We wanted the design to harmonize with the lay of the land, with minimal compromise to the terrain. She recommended a well-respected builder of log homes who has a heart and passion for his craft."

"That's obvious," Maggie said. "This place is a show-stopper."

Larkin filled a kettle with water and put it on the back burner. She brought a small wicker basket of tea bags over to the granite-topped island. Maggie slid onto a tall chair, hooking her long legs around the lower rungs.

"It took just shy of two years to build it, from the excavation to the front door mat. We love it here, Maggie. The house was nearing completion when you did what you called 'going dark,' dropping out of sight for a space of time."

Outside the kitchen window, a blurred frenzy of red feathers announced an attack waged against the squirrel stuffing his face at the bird feeder. The squirrel's fast retreat left the feeder swinging, dumping seeds onto the ground.

Into the growing silence, Larkin spoke just above a whisper. "We were so afraid we'd lost you, dear child. We were nearly frantic. When you finally called, we thanked the Lord for bringing you through that murky vale and back to us."

Over a period of three years, Maggie's worldview had suffered very heavy psychological tolls, accumulating about a twelve on her emotional ten-point Richter scale.

"Dark. Yes, I had to retreat," Maggie recalled. "The end of the world, like everyone predicted, didn't happen. However …"

Her best friend was killed in a blazing car crash. Julie was fleeing for her life, running away from her physically abusive husband.

The fixed-rent apartment complex where Maggie had been living for several years was to become a parking lot. She had had fifteen days to relocate.

Her beloved furry companion, an ancient tabby cat, Toby TumTum, went to Catnip Heaven.

"The pivotal point was the bank robbery," Maggie said, finishing her narrative. "You probably read about it. It hit the AP newswire."

Larkin turned on her stool, facing Maggie.

Robbers had burst into the lobby of the bank where she was working. "Unaware of the drama unfolding out front, I was just about to step out of the ladies' room when I heard gunshots." With the detachment of time between the event back then and the telling of it now, Maggie related the story.

"Davey had wanted to switch our lunch break times. His girlfriend went to lunch at one o'clock. It was Valentine's Day, and he was so excited. He showed me the ring: a tiny diamond in a simple old-fashioned setting." She smiled at the sweet sentimentality, and then sobered.

"Since no one was in the lobby, I locked my money drawer and the computer screen. As I walked past the front windows, I saw a junky old car parked in the space right in front of the doors. That it even had a vanity plate struck me funny: TOO BAD. Two men wearing grungy, paint-streaked clothes got out of the car. Workers came in on Fridays to cash their paychecks, so I didn't think much about it."

The teakettle whistled, startling them both. After they chose teabags from the basket, Larkin poured the hot water into their mugs. While the tea was steeping, Maggie continued her saga.

"When I heard the shots, I froze. I waited a lifetime with my hand on the door." For what, she didn't know. "I have never been so flat-out scared."

"Mercy, child!" Larkin patted Maggie's arm, her voice full of the compassion that only a Southern-born lady can convey in the space of two words.

A century or two later she heard sirens. The police found her, sitting on the counter beside the sink staring into the middle distance.

Maggie was taken to her supervisor's office, the temporary Command Central. She related her story to him and the police, and repeated it more times than she could count.

"Right then, my emotional bell hit Tilt and I pitched the metaphoric hammer to the tattooed barker. I gathered up my purse, handed my keys to my supervisor, said 'I quit,' and high-tailed it out of Dodge. Well, it was Tucson, actually." She took a careful sip of the very hot tea.

She had cashed her paycheck and drew five hundred dollars out of savings to go with it. After notifying her landlord, she put all of her meager belongings in a long-term storage facility, and sent a check to her car insurance carrier for two-year coverage.

"I threw some clothes, two boxes of books, and my

guitar in the back seat of my poor old car. I left Tucson and drove northward with no destination in mind. I ended up in northeastern Arizona. The little roadside restaurant where I stopped for lunch had a 'Waitress Wanted' sign in the window. I handed the sign to the man behind the counter and asked, 'Where's my apron?' He pointed to the linen shelf, and I had me a job."

* * * * *

The man was the owner, Jake Owenson. He liked her spunk and no-nonsense attitude. "She can handle the truckers, tourists, and transients, and give back verbal change," he told his wife later that first evening. He smiled a tobacco-stained grin at Maggie as she set down their dinner plates. She returned the smile.

The restaurant was a hopeful addition to an unpretentious motel sitting on a patch of Arizona desert beside a lonesome highway in a no-name town. In return for doing her own housekeeping, Maggie's room was rent-free. Working overtime without extra pay, just to stay busy, she had all of her meals and whatever coffee, tea, or soft drink she wanted.

She relied on cash for her few incidentals and more books. Since she didn't use her credit card and had no personal telephone, there were no bills to pay. She hadn't tried to vanish. Anyone with a lick of sense could have found her. Maybe.

She sidestepped nosy questions.

"Where ya from?"

"Not here," she answered.

Some folks were more persistent. "How long you here

71

for?"

"The restaurant closes at nine every night except Sunday."

"What are you doing here?"

"Bringing you your lunch."

Three months later, right before Memorial Day, Maggie became restless, a sure sign that she was healing. She prayed every day to the Lord who had never abandoned her, and never would, even when her world had collapsed around her ears.

Jake Owenson bragged long afterward that Maggie was the best waitress that little restaurant ever had.

* * * * *

"I said goodbye to the Owensons, who said they were mighty sorry to see me go. Then I put Arizona in my rearview mirror and headed vaguely eastward. My car broke down in Oklahoma City. I took that as a sign I was supposed to stop there. Since I was bent on picking my life up again in a brand new town," Maggie shrugged, "it was as good a place as any." She idly folded the paper napkin into a tiny square.

Several noisy cardinals were perched on the feeder. They scattered in a flurry of red when a raucous blue jay landed in their midst. Within moments, a battalion of cardinals descended on the jay's head in retaliation. He took off, chattering his opinion of their deplorable manners.

"Then I answered a want ad for a writer and public relations wizard at Allgood's Advertising Agency. In the interview, I told Frances Allgood that I would be the best copywriter they would ever hire. Wonder of wonders, out of ninety-five applicants, I got the job." She sipped the cooling tea.

She made a down payment on a modest 1940s bungalow in one of Oklahoma City's bedroom communities. "I exchanged the tranquil desert for the strangulation of city dwelling. My poor, tired car was undependable. I traded it for a small Ford pickup. Made a quick run to Arizona to get my things out of storage. Then I called you."

"We were so relieved, Maggie dear." Larkin finished her tea and set the cup down on a napkin.

"I had this increasingly urgent feeling to call you. It reached the point where I couldn't ignore it any longer, so I picked up the phone." Maggie folded her arms as if she were cold.

Larkin put the teakettle back on the burner. "And not a moment too soon, dear. That day was the end of our stay in North Belgrade. We were all packed and ready to go. The phone was to be disconnected the very next day. That nudging was the Holy Spirit."

Maggie smiled at her beloved aunt. "I am very glad I listened and responded."

"And we are, too. Believe it, Maggie. We love you as much as if you were our own."

I wish I were your very own, Maggie thought, surprised at the truth in her reaction to her aunt's statement.

Afterward, they had stayed in touch by way of emails and intermittent phone calls. And now, at last, five years later, Maggie was sitting in their cheerful kitchen.

Whatcha gonna do, Maggie Storm Blue?

The screaming teakettle startled Maggie out of her abstraction. "More tea? Yes, please."

"Heavy weather, child. Rod and I are eternally grateful, and thankful that you rode out that storm. We knew the will of God would never take you where His grace would not protect you." Larkin returned with the teakettle. "We prayed for you, knowing eventually that you would call us."

"You folks are the only family I have. Any that I claim, anyway," she amended. "And I love you right back!"

Sloshing her tea bag up and down in the hot water, she turned her personal page and scanned the impersonal newspaper's page. Peering intently into the tea mug like she was looking for an answer in its depths, Maggie decided the brew had steeped long enough, and took a sip. She went back to reading the paper.

"Hrumpf, the job situation here isn't very inspiring."

Siam sprang up onto the island and Larkin pushed him off. "No! I do declare, Siam, you have the manners of a redneck. Go chase Sheba, you scamp." The cat flicked his tail and sashayed into the Lake Room.

"Looking for work here, are you?"

"Always curious," Maggie answered, depositing her limp tea bag in a saucer. "Most jobs want people with PC software abilities, and I'm a 'Mac' gal."

Recalling Siam's delight in chasing the bedclothes every morning, she said, "Regrettably, knowing how to make up a bed with a cat still in it doesn't quite qualify as an additional marketable life experience," she said. "No, I will stay put until God moves me. Nevertheless, I must do my part and keep my ear to the ground."

"True. He opens doors but does expect us to step over the thresholds. Speaking of which, Rita, our Realtor friend, called yesterday. She mentioned a nice Cape Cod cottage on Cranberry Lane that has just come on the market."

Maggie nodded acknowledgment of Larkin's statement. She had no intention of answering the implied question, at least not yet. Often, over the course of the past five years, her relatives had urged her to chuck the hassle in Oklahoma and to move back home to Maine.

Maggie considered her fingernails. Her French manicure looked frazzled. "Where do you get your nails done?"

"At the Hair-Doux. My appointment is for this afternoon at three, for manicure and a haircut. I want to look my best for the Shindig."

"Does she do gel or acrylic nails? I need gel. Could she fit me in, too?"

"Her nail gal does both. I'll call right now, Serena may have an opening."

"Fine by me," Maggie replied. "Thanks."

11

Maggie, It's Shindig Time!

Wednesday, July 4th, late morning

"HERE, MAGGIE, CATCH! You're on oven duty." Larkin tossed the words over her shoulder at the same time she tossed an apron. Maggie caught it and headed for the stove, tying the garment as she went.

The sun was shining in fits and starts, playing hide-and-seek with benevolent clouds, promising a nice day for the fifth annual Fourth of July Shindig. A fresh breeze coming off the lake helped to keep the unwelcome flying insects at bay.

The festivities wouldn't officially start for hours yet. Already hoards of people were bustling about, getting ready. An appreciated set crew of dedicated volunteers came every year to help. Without them, the Richardsons alone could not have managed the magnitude to which this annual production had grown.

Lively chatter and cautionary yells punctuated the air. Men from the Elks Lodge manned the cookers while the women unwrapped the meats and jostled platters. The younger Boy Scouts put up food tables. The older Scouts marked off the parking areas with temporary posts and rope. Ladies from the church took care of organizing the who-brings-what for side dishes, desserts, and beverages. The table covers and decorations were the purview of the Girl Scouts. The volunteer firefighters undertook the massive task of the day-after cleanup.

Certain dishes were traditional with Larkin, and the aromas floating about in her kitchen were mouth-watering. "The brownies smell almost done. Put the apple pies in next, please, dear." She hummed "Dixie" while she bustled about.

In the spacious utility room, Larkin opened the linen closet door and extracted a stack of plastic tablecloths. Festive with patriotic colors, the white background was printed with dancing red, gold, and blue stars. "The Scouts are helping Rod unload the tables from the pastor's truck. I'll take these out now so the girls can start dressing the tables." She headed for the door and almost tripped over the dog.

"Anything else?"

"Oh, shoo Sheba out, will you, dear? She's right underfoot."

"Where's Siam?"

"Upstairs, hiding. He hates crowds. Too noisy."

Maggie retrieved a bag of steak bones from the freezer, pulled one out and coaxed Sheba outside. She returned to the kitchen just as the oven timer rang.

The heat blast rising from the open oven door ruffled her bangs, bringing with it the decadent aroma of warm chocolate. "Yum!"

She set the four pans of double-fudge brownies on wire racks to cool, then turned the oven temperature up to 425 degrees. From the refrigerator, she removed the apple pies and slipped off their plastic covers. She wrapped strips of foil around the edges to prevent the pastry from becoming too crispy before the pies were cooked through.

Immediately following a sunrise-early breakfast, Larkin had handed Maggie six bags of Granny Smith apples and an apple peeler, which made short work of an otherwise onerous job. She fixed the apples while Larkin made the pastry. Three of the pies had dried cranberries and chopped walnuts added to them; the other three were plain apple. All were steeped in a rich mixture of butter, cinnamon, and nutmeg.

Her aunt's apple pies were hot items at her church's bake sales. No one could figure out what made hers so special, the extra ingredients that made all the difference. She cautioned Maggie to keep that mixture's secret close to the vest. "Otherwise, my pies won't win ribbons at the county fair." Generous pats of creamery butter were dotted atop the apples before the top crust was fitted.

Give her a party and Larkin had a plan. Maggie acquiesced without a murmur of protest to Larkin's crisp orders. She was convinced that her aunt should have been a professional party planner instead of a seller of antiques.

A young man breezed into the kitchen, carrying a watermelon sliced lengthwise and wrapped in white paper. "Here ya go, Miz Richardson," he said, setting the melon on the counter near the sink and removing the paper. "Lemme know if there's anything else you need help with, okay?" He tossed the soggy paper into the large trash barrel that had been brought in from the garage to catch the bulk of the day's detritus.

"I will. Thank you, Jerry," she called to his retreating

back.

The oven-ready bell rang. She shipped each of the six pies into the spacious oven, shut the oven door, and set the timer.

Larkin slashed the juicy red watermelon meat into squares and carefully scooped out the chunks, placing them in a colander in the sink to drain. She scraped the two melon hulls clean.

Maggie went to the refrigerator for the bowls of honeydew and cantaloupe chunks that had arrived earlier. She dumped the melons into the prepared watermelon boats, and covered them with plastic wrap.

"Beyond your formal invitations, who all typically come?"

"Chad and Autumn said they were coming, along with her sister, Summer, and their families. Most of the people you met last night at worship team practice, and some from the baby shower, if you'll remember any of them."

While transferring the rich, dark chocolate squares to a large plastic platter, a brownie broke and fell onto the countertop. "Oops, one for the kitchen helper!" Maggie picked up the runaway brownie and took a bite. Licking her fingers, she made purring sounds relative to chocolate ecstasy. "These are so-o-o good."

Washing her hands at the kitchen sink, Maggie said, "I ran into Cousin Victor at Bob Morgan's funeral. Rather, he ran into me. Right 'smarmy,' he is, to quote Autumn." She gave her aunt the condensed version of their brief encounter. "I hope he's not coming."

"I am not about to invite Victor. He may well show up,

though. With the gates wide open, people do tend to pop in and out. I agree with Autumn's assessment. From what little I do know about him, his source of income is highly suspect. He has the morals of an alligator and as much charm as a scorpion. I hope that little piss-ant has slithered back under his rock in New York or somewhere, anywhere other than here."

Surprised at Larkin's use of even a mild Southern cuss word, Maggie snickered. "If we were to talk about his manners, it wouldn't be a long conversation."

"Very true, dear," Larkin agreed.

"If he lives in New York, what's he doing here?"

"Summering, I presume," Larkin answered. "Most of the cabins over by Loon Creek are seasonal rentals."

A burly man wearing faded Dickies and a plaid cotton shirt with the sleeves rolled up to his elbows walked in, carrying a wheel of cheese. "Hey, Larkin. Gotcha some of this Vermont sharp cheddar. Where d'yer want it?"

"Oh, thank you, Charlie." Larkin took a large cutting board from the rack and laid it down on the counter near the sink. "Right here, please."

"Want me to chunk it for yer? It's a some ol' big un."

"Would you, please? Bless your heart. Just in eighths, then we can manage it." She handed him a long, heavy bladed, very serious knife. Charlie's strong arms and big hands went at it, making the job look so easy.

"There you be. Anythin' else?"

Being fully assured that all was well, he lumbered off. Larkin selected two more heavy knives and cutting boards. She and Maggie chatted while they cut the aromatic cheese wedges into thick slices.

Maggie went to the utility room, returning with several large plastic plates. "Well, if Victor drops in, would my sisters come, too?"

"It's always possible. Like I said before, after your mother died and they went to live with Aunt June, we had little news about them. They all grew up together, so Victor may know where they are now."

"First there was Beryl, who's four years younger than me."

"You were still living in Weeks Mills with your mother when Beryl was born, right?"

"Yes. I don't know why, but right after that I went to live with Grandmother and Grandfather on Deer Hill. It was the spring before I started school. That summer we moved to North Belgrade."

"Your birthday fell such that when school opened, you were still four, if I remember correctly?"

"Quite right. I squeaked in under the cutoff date, which made me almost the baby of the class." She arranged thick slices of the rich orange-yellow cheese onto the plate, placing sheets of waxed paper between the layers.

"Amber came along two years later. I was nine when the youngest was born. Ruby was sweet, at least when she was a baby. I never understood the dynamics in that family," Maggie said. "I'm quite sure Ruby didn't try to give me heart failure by putting a revulsion of spiders in my mailbox." She shuddered. "Hate them things!"

"I've never heard of 'revulsion' as a lexicographic collective term for spiders," Larkin said, attending to her own plate of cheese slices.

"There isn't one that I'm aware of, so I made it up."

"Well spoken, my dear. I don't care much for them either. But whoever would have done a mean thing like that to you?" Larkin's soft voice echoed outrage along with compassion.

"I have a strong suspicion that it was Beryl. And I'm right convinced that later, she tried to seriously harm me." She hesitated, saying in an undertone, "Maybe she really meant to *kill* me."

Larkin's blue eyes went wide with alarm. "Really, dear, when was that?"

"In the late nineteen-sixties. Kiernan and I had been married only a few months. This was before we moved to Tucson. He had just shipped out for his first tour in Vietnam, and I was home alone. Uncharacteristically, the girls dropped in for a visit. The next day, I was about to take a big box down to the cellar when something made me hesitate."

"Oh, dear!"

"Just in time, I stopped. Several dowel rods were scattered on the third stair down. Those were very steep stairs. Had I stepped on the rods, I would have slipped and landed on the stone floor. Sisters like that," she concluded, "I do *not* need."

Larkin rinsed her knife in the sink and returned to cut more cheese. "Mercy me! I didn't know about that, dear. How mean-spirited and vicious." She shook her head in dismay at the inhumanity of mankind. "Curious, isn't it, how children of the same family can each turn out so differently," Larkin mused. "I thought the world of John and Hannah

Richardson. Your grandparents were salt-of-the-earth people. Amos was the oldest, then came June, Rod, and Marion, each about four years apart. Amos and Marion died a long time ago. I hear June's not in very good health these days. Rod's the only one of their children who fell close to the tree."

"I vaguely recall going to Deer Hill to live with my grandparents. Memories of those early years are real fuzzy." Maggie popped a crumb of cheese into her mouth.

"Marion divorced Edward Harlan in 1952. Then she married Elroy Gholson. Beryl was born in early 1954, I believe," Larkin said. "That was the last time we heard from Marion."

"Marion brought the baby home. Shortly thereafter, it was like she slammed a door in my face. I never did understand it. She demanded that I call her 'Marion' instead of 'Mom' then." Maggie stopped to fan cheese slices on the plate.

"Marion wasn't your uncle's favorite sister either, Maggie." Larkin covered the cheese with plastic wrap. "We get a card from June only at Christmas, no letter."

Unable to come up with an appropriate comment on that statement, Maggie went to the sink and rinsed her cheese-encrusted knife. "At first, I hated Marion, but hate requires too much negative energy. Then I had no feelings for her, or for my sisters, for that matter."

"I imagine," Larkin agreed, sympathizing as only a Southern-bred lady can do. She brought out a box of crackers and two small plates.

Maggie filled two glasses with ice water while Larkin cut

small wedges of cheese for each of them.

Larkin slid onto a tall stool and sighed. "We need a break and I just cannot wait another minute to have some of this wonderful cheese," she said, taking a bite of the aromatic chunk.

"It is very good," Maggie concurred. "I have to go to a specialty store in Oklahoma City to find good cheese."

"We are blessed that Charlie Baker carries it. He owns the Mercantile. Every year he generously donates a wheel of cheese for our Shindig. It never lasts long."

Swallowing a big gulp of water, Maggie returned to her reminisces. "Grandfather never said much, but he once told me that he and Grandmother took over the raising of me gladly. Blessing, that. We'd visit Marion every summer for four weeks, and over Christmas vacation, just Grandmother and me. For whatever reason, Grandfather refused to set foot in Marion's house. I simply dreaded those visits. Marion tolerated me on sufferance only because her mother was there."

"More fool, she. You know, my dear, God always watches over His own. He's had His hand on your shoulder since the day you were born, and before." Larkin took their plates over to the sink and rinsed them before putting them in the dishwasher.

"Quite right. With all of those confusing undercurrents, I was grateful for Grandmother's physical presence, though."

Larkin glanced at the clock. "Oh, my! Look at the time!" A melodious five-note chime sounded. "That's the north kitchen door. Answer it, will you, dear?" she asked just as the timer beeped. She opened the oven door and began removing the pies to cooling racks.

12

Maggie Meets Strangers

Wednesday, July 4th, late afternoon

THE WOMAN STANDING ON THE TOP STEP wore red cotton slacks and a blue-and-white striped long-sleeved tunic. A broad smile pushed her cheeks up like a chipmunk's in a kind face beginning to show some weathering.

"If that's what I think it is," Maggie said, pointing to the plate of dark-dark chocolate fudge the woman held, "you could get mugged before you ever make it to the dessert table. By me!"

The fudge maker beamed and turned sideways to the two tall men standing on the step below her. The very tall, big-bear man had quarterback-wide shoulders and a physique to match. He sported an old-fashioned handlebar mustache. Coming from the large ceramic roasting pan he carried was the unmistakable fragrance of honest-to-goodness Boston baked beans, not the kind out of a can.

The other man of almost equal stature wore pressed jeans, a blue Western-style shirt, a summer-weight Stetson hat, and boots – worn, genuine cowboy boots. Maggie grinned in appreciation of the vision of mature Western masculinity. Slung over his shoulder was a serious-looking camera case. He carried a large cardboard box chock-full of jumbo bags of potato chips.

"Hi, Maggie," the big-bear man said, smiling. "The Colonel about?"

Blinking in surprise, she thought, *Of course they know who I am.*

It's the small-town know-everyone facts of life. Efficient to a fault, was the news-vine. Larkin had said that Birdie Mandrill's news-vine was far more detailed than any daily paper. Baysinger Cove was the kind of town where the root of the vine would know everything within two hours. The local newspaper printed all the news that missed being libelous, while Birdie spread the slanderous.

"Um, yeah. Uncle Rod is down by the lake, or thereabouts."

"Ayuh, we'll find him. Thanks."

Maggie hurried back to the kitchen. She took the hot pies over to the island. Larkin organized her kitchen in a systematic and logical order. Most of her rationale made sense to Maggie, though once in a while she was stumped.

"Let me see, if I were a pie server, I would be …"

Of course, the fancy servers were in one of the drawers of the kitchen island cabinets. Therefore, plastic servers should be with the picnic supplies in the utility room closet. "Aha!"

She had just finished cutting the last pie into eight wedges when three women of varying heights, sizes, and dispositions came in.

"Hi, Maggie, give us those pies. Gina and Mavis'll come back for the cheese," said the woman wearing a red-checked apron, the obvious captain of this requisition team. They headed out single-file, each woman carrying two pies wrapped in towels.

First thing this morning, Maggie had tied a red bandanna over her hair. Untying it, she eased the strands that were entangled in the knot. She pulled the bandanna off and shook out her hair, glad to be free of the confining triangle of cloth.

Gina and Mavis returned the towels and picked up the cheese plates. Maggie followed them out. Her past experience waitressing was a boon now. She hefted the heavy platter of brownies out to the large white tent pavilion where the food tables were set up.

"Yo-o-o, Maggie! Over here! I want you to meet some folks." Rod's voice carried over the music and laughter. The three kitchen-door people were gathered around her uncle.

"Be right there!"

The dessert table was loaded with a plethora of delicious choices. Maggie pushed several of the plates and bowls closer together, making room for the brownies. A second table was dedicated to pies and was just as crowded.

There had to be a good two hundred or more people here already. Judging by the hum of engines and car doors slamming, folks were still arriving. Bless Aunt Larkin's party-loving heart − she must have sent out a blanket "Y'all Come!"

Rod put his arm around her shoulders, drawing her closer to him. In that eloquent, simple gesture, Maggie began to understand that she belonged here in the Richardson family circle. Attendant to that realization came a wave of sadness that surprised her. She was too distracted now to explore why.

"This is Walker Bainbridge, and his wife, Abigail. Walker is our sheriff, and Abigail owns the quilt shop. And CJ Dubois, here, is our photographer extraordinaire. Friends, this is my niece, Maggie."

During pleasantries and howdys, Maggie trotted out her meeting-strangers lady manners. CJ took her hand and held it a year longer than Emily Post would have approved.

"How-do, Miss Maggie. I'm very pleased to meet you," he said, his deep voice full of nuances and a hint of laughter.

Dark brown eyes stared down into Maggie's green eyes and sent shivery fingers riffling through the pages of her musty memory, stirring up little more than fusty dust motes. *Hmmm, he looks like, no, it can't be,* she thought. *An old-time Western movie hero, maybe? Clint Walker as Cheyenne Bodie? Razzlefratz, I hate this fuzzy memory thing!*

Abigail Bainbridge stepped away from the menfolk and rescued Maggie's hand. Her very short light brown hair was gel-spiked into full attention. "Are you a quilter, Maggie? Larkin said you're both coming to the Society meeting on Friday."

Warming to the gentle spirit that contradicted the prickly exterior, Maggie walked to the beverage table with Abigail. "Yes, we are. I'm not a quilter in the true sense of the word. In the bad old days I have made many so-called sane quilts. My focus now is on the art side of quilting, more eclectic."

At Abigail's encouraging nod, Maggie continued. "More specifically, my passion is all about crazy quilts. No rules in my world."

"I understand! Our Quilt Society is not insular in our thinking. With seventy-five members and growing, we may be small, but we're mighty! We have satellite groups, 'Circles,' we call them, that gather outside of the Society meeting days. We have traditional quilters, appliqué lovers, and art-related circles. I'm seeing a growing interest in crazy quilts, too. Naturally, Larkin leads the Crazy Quilt Circle."

"This little town continues to surprise me. There's so much going on here. Now, what do you have in your shop, Miss Abigail?"

To help control the inevitable spills, the beverage table was set up in a grassy area beside the screened food tent. Abigail held a plastic tumbler under the spigot of the pink lemonade cooler and flipped the lever. One eyebrow was cocked a bit higher, giving her an air of perpetual amusement.

"Well, you'll just have to come by the shop and see, right?" she teased, warm brown eyes twinkling.

The strident notes of the come-to-dinner triangle pierced the air. Abigail hooked Maggie's arm. "C'mon, Maggie, they're gathering on the south shore for the blessing and the flag salute. Then we'll eat. I'm starved, aren't you?"

13

Maggie Sees Fireworks and Sparks

Wednesday, July 4th, evening

THE SHINDIG WAS IN FULL SWING. Laughter and chatter wove through the toe-tapping country music and soft rock melodies, amplifying the festive atmosphere. The gentle breezes from the lake helped to temper the summer heat. The tangy, sharp overtone of salt water was a sensory reminder that the Atlantic Ocean was just a few miles beyond Old Man Mountain.

Rod and his friend who owned the hardware store, Wayne Hardy, cornered Maggie at the dessert table. Rod was finishing with the fulsome introductions when he was called away.

Wayne and Maggie engaged in idle small talk, the kind of polite chitchat that surfaces when one has nothing to say to the other, and find no common ground on which to stake a meaningful conversation. Maggie was dredging up Quick Getaway Polite Excuse Number Seventeen when a man wearing vivid purple plaid Bermuda shorts, a garish orange and green Hawaiian shirt, blue-striped socks, and red high-top tennis shoes, pranced up to them.

He laid a proprietary hand on Wayne's arm, whispered in his ear, and then glared at Maggie. Wayne inclined his head and made his excuses. He walked off holding hands with his fashion-challenged partner.

"Sorry, Uncle Rod, but that ship won't sail with me on it," she said under her breath to their retreating backs.

She filled her dessert plate and found an empty seat beside Autumn. Chad and Autumn chattered about the many members of their extended family. Maggie listened with half an ear as she finished a piece of Larkin's pie. While she loved her oldest friend, and liked people in general, Maggie also craved peace. Solitude was where she recharged her emotional batteries. She left the table and tossed her paper plate in one of the many strategically placed big oil barrels that were standing in as trash receptacles tonight.

Light breezes drifted in off the lake, ruffling Maggie's hair. She turned to face the refreshing breeze. Wanting to escape from the din's epicenter for a few minutes, she also hoped for a brief respite from meeting folks whom she would never remember.

Meandering in the general direction of the south tip of the peninsula toward the boat dock, Maggie dodged groups of people engaged in animated conversation punctuated with guffaws and giggles, shouts and salutations, and couples dancing on the grass.

Before she had gone very far, a man detached himself from a knot of people. He swaggered up to her. Behind him was a big man who could have been an NFL linebacker in a previous profession. In spite of the scars on his face that attested to other confrontations, he didn't look threatening.

Oh, bless me, it's Victor again. What's he doing here?

The boorish Victor stood as tall as his short frame

allowed, with added height gained from his tassel-loafer elevator shoes. Standing with legs akimbo, his puffed-out bantam rooster chest emphasized the start of a beer belly paunch under the lavender pullover shirt.

"Hey, Maggie?" He spoke around a wad of tobacco in his cheek. In a macho move, he hiked his chinos up on scrawny hips.

She grimaced, resigning herself to the interruption. "I suspect so."

Remembering the much younger version of this older man, she said, "Looks like age hasn't housebroken *you*."

A strong breeze lifted the wave of his artfully draped, dyed dark brown hair, revealing a small scar on his wrinkled left temple. Maggie remembered bestowing that memento. It was Christmas morning, 1953. Nine-year-old Victor had taken her brand-new, highly prized red wagon filled with A-B-C blocks away from her and claimed it for his own. Ignoring four-year-old Maggie's tearful pleading, he had no intention of relinquishing it to its rightful owner.

She was an even-tempered, shy little girl. But when wedged into a corner, she gave back as good as she got, or better. Waiting her chance, she had beaned him with one of the blocks. Its sharp edge left an inch-long scar.

The red wagon was one of her precious treasures, currently residing in her Oklahoma bungalow with her fifty-year-old teddy bear riding shotgun.

"What are you doing here anyway?" Victor asked. "You're not wanted. You're here just to butter up to Uncle Rod so you can walk away with everything. Just remember, dear cousin, it's not all about *you*. You aren't the only one in line for the goods. Back off … or else."

"Or else *what*? Are you threatening me? *You*? Get real."

"That ain't no threat. I'm just warnin' you, cuz. Go back home where you belong." He spiked the sentence with one of the most common, foulest words to ever disgrace the English language.

"You have a sewer mouth, Victor. Your words need laundering on the heavy cycle with several cups of bleach."

He spat on the ground and took a step nearer. "When you fly home, don't forget your broomstick."

"Leave, *mister*," she said. "Now."

Victor's first mistake was to step in front of her. His second mistake was to threaten her. Quicker than think, old man Victor was flat on his back on the rough ground. He groaned and coughed in between unoriginal, repetitive swear words.

Maggie stepped back from him, rubbing her hands on her jeans like she was trying to remove the grime from having touched him. Glancing around, she noticed a crowd had gathered to watch the small drama. They were clapping, laughing, and cheering, so maybe she wasn't in *too* much trouble. The linebacker dude was snickering, too.

Footsteps coming up fast behind her announced company coming.

"I sure hope it's the cavalry," she murmured.

It was.

"Got a problem here, Maggie?"

"Victor is just leaving, thank you, Walker."

"I'll make sure he does," the sheriff answered, reaching down to grab Victor's bony hand.

"She made me almost swallow my chaw!" Victor spat out a brown stream, barely missing Maggie's foot. He glared first at her then at the sheriff. "She coulda hurt me."

"You heard the lady. Leave, *mister*."

Maggie recognized the intent behind CJ's particular inflection of the word. If you were in Texas and someone called you *mister* like that, you might want to consider settling up your bar tab and moseying on outta there.

"Aw right, I'm going. I'm going!" He turned and stumbled toward the parking area, shoving people out of his way with the big dude dogging his heels.

Walker turned to Maggie. "Where did you learn that move?" he asked.

"Are you a black belt or something else we might should know about?" CJ asked Texas-style.

"Hardly," she answered. "Last winter I took a six-week self-defense class for older women. The cop teaching it was a good ole boy who kept calling me 'Little Lady.' I didn't like his condescending attitude and told him to quit. He didn't let up. So, one day in class, I flipped him."

"Then what happened?" CJ asked. "Did someone go your bail?"

Maggie shook her head. "After that he called me 'Ma'am.' But I never turned my back on him, just in case."

Both men burst out laughing. Well, it was funny, in retrospect, so she laughed with them.

"He's real bad news, Maggie," the sheriff said. "Not sure what he's up to, here. He's renting old man Watson's cabin, the last one on Blue Jay Lane. You'd best stay away from him."

"Cousin Victor? He just acts tough. I'm not scared of him."

"Just be careful, Maggie. He's dangerous." The sheriff's cell phone rang. "Got to run. Later."

CJ took Maggie's hand and said, "Let's go watch the fireworks. The ones over the lake, I mean."

14

Maggie Sees More Sparks

Wednesday, July 4th, late evening

"**WHERE ARE WE HEADED, CJ?**" Maggie shrugged the cloth tote bag back up on her shoulder.

"Just up here a ways to that break in the pine trees. It's a great vantage point for spectacular sunset shots and a clear view of the fireworks. No overhanging limbs to interfere, of trees or people." CJ shifted his camera case and switched a small drink cooler to his other hand.

They were heading to the western side of the peninsula, to an area northwest of the temporary dance pavilion. The soft pine needle carpet muffled their footsteps. She could see the tall wrought iron fence where it met with the rocky edge of the lake on the northwest side of the peninsula. Only a mountain goat could navigate those sharp granite boulders.

They came to the small clearing where two wrought iron and cedar plank park benches faced the lake. CJ set his camera case on one bench and the cooler under the seat.

"Rod put these benches here the first year they hosted the Shindig. We sat here and watched the fireworks in peace."

"Aunt Larkin didn't mention that she and Uncle Rod would be joining us tonight."

"Probably not." CJ chuckled. "This whole Shindig thing

has gone beyond her earliest speculations."

The balmy night was fast closing down. The food had been plentiful and delicious. If folks had gone away hungry, well, they were just too dad-blamed fussy. After taking a break to eat, the band had started up again. The never-say-die dancers were still at it.

Tripping the light fantastic on the grass, the wood-slatted decks, or the temporary dance pavilion was a long distance from the ease of a fast dance floor. Maggie's dogs were barking and she was looking forward to a nice long sit-down. She dropped her tote on the ground beside her.

"As busy as they are tonight, I hope they at least stop long enough to see the show."

A light breeze ruffled her hair and set the branches of the pine trees to waving a shy welcome. Wheeling seagulls danced on the wind currents, diving low to catch a late dinner.

Maggie sat with her hands in her lap, palms upward. She smelled the heady brine and watched the waves of Horseshoe Lake caressing the rocky shore. Listening to the cry of the gulls and the hooting owl, she waxed nostalgic. Her heavy sigh was for the not-quite-forgotten memory, emphasizing her underlying homesickness for Maine.

CJ reached in his pocket and pulled out a handful of change.

Maggie jerked out of her brown study when he dropped a penny into her palm.

"Oh!"

"Well?"

She turned the dull copper coin over, checking the

reverse side out of habit. "If salt brine and the stench of seaweed at low tide can make me homesick, well ... my dilemma is, do I want to be here in Maine, where I grew up, or in Oklahoma, where I live now?"

It wasn't a coveted wheat penny to add to her collection, so she returned the coin. Maggie slid off the bench and picked her way over the rocks leading down to the water. Too many years had gone by since she last hopped rocks, and she was a lot older now. The art came back to her, like riding a bicycle, but caution prevailed. That she was wearing sandals was also a major consideration. She stepped onto a large flat stone and stopped.

Across the lake, several colorful lakeside cottages dotted the landscape, tucked here and there amid green pines and blue cedars. In the distance, people looked like little dolls moving around. Rod had mentioned that this side of the horseshoe-shaped lake was a mile across. The eastern side was three-quarters of a mile wide and bumped up against Old Man Mountain. The southern curve at its longest point was three miles wide.

She heard CJ approaching though he did not do any rock hopping to join her. Boots were not conducive to the sport any more than her sandals were.

"What's to keep you there in Oklahoma?"

"A job, with whatever security *that* provides. There's my cozy bungalow, which I really like. Friends. You know, the usual ties." She started back, making her way across the rocks to meet him on the gravel path.

"Any family?" he asked, taking her hand.

"The only family I claim live right here on this property."

Maggie hoped to forestall any more questions on that subject. She didn't want to dredge that old, tiresome baggage up again tonight. Spending time with CJ was special ... and precious, she realized with a start. *Where'd that thought come from? He's practically a stranger!* She shivered.

"Um, let's go back, CJ. I need a wrap."

Holding hands, they made their way up the graveled path. They settled down on the bench. From her tote bag, Maggie pulled out a lightweight silk-wool knitted shawl and slipped the garment around her shoulders.

The fireworks celebration was scheduled to begin sometime around ten o'clock tonight. The Town Council had squeezed their budget to accommodate a full hour of pyrotechnics to be shot over Horseshoe Lake. Maggie thought the poor waterfowl and other critters that lived in the area would be deafened unless they headed north at the first volley.

People milled around, putting down blankets and setting up lawn chairs on the lower sandy shoreline near the wharf and boat dock. Peals of laughter and music carried across the increasing darkness.

Maggie carefully removed a plastic container from her tote bag. She set it on the ground beside the opposite bench.

"What's that?"

"A homemade mosquito trap. Larkin researched it on the Internet. She made one and decided we should be the first to try it out."

Before heading out, they had slathered themselves with a second dose of a natural, eco-friendly, homemade mosquito and no-see-um midge repellent. "Midges have a wicked bite totally disproportionate to their size. I hope this gizmo will attract them, too."

Larkin had cut a liter soda bottle in half and poured in the potion. The top was flipped and inserted funnel down in the bottom half. The black tape kept the two parts together.

"What's in it?"

"Water, brown sugar, and yeast. Black is the color skeeters are drawn to, supposedly."

"Does it work?"

"I guess. The potion creates carbon dioxide, which attracts the bloodsuckers. I hope this keeps them occupied enough so they leave us alone. We'll soon see." She set it on the ground behind their bench.

"Is that why you're wearing white tonight?" CJ asked.

"That, and psychologically it's cooler."

They sat in companionable silence, relaxing in the rugged beauty that surrounded them, watching twilight creep away and night crawl in. The trees seemed to meld and grow closer in the dimming light, clustering together to whisper the day's secrets to one another.

"Where are you from, Maggie? I can't place your accent."

"I grew up here. After I married Kiernan Blue, we moved to Arizona. Five years ago I relocated to Oklahoma. My Yankee accent melted somewhere along the way."

"Divorced?"

"No. Near the end of his second tour of Viet Nam, Kiernan was killed. I never remarried. You?"

"I'm a widower."

In the increasing silence, Maggie sensed they needed a

change of subject.

"What kind of photography is your specialty?" She leaned forward to inspect his camera case.

"The serious side is forensic. I stumbled into that by chance, or as I believe, by Divine appointment. The Franklin County, Texas, forensic photographer and I are good friends. Paul and I went on nature photo shoots together whenever we could get away." He slouched down on the bench seat and crossed his ankles.

"There was a traffic accident with fatalities, but Paul was vacationing in France. He had suggested to the Texas State Police that they call me if something came up while he was away."

"That must have been right gruesome," Maggie commented with an involuntary shudder of revulsion.

"Yes, it was, yet it was fascinating. That's when I went for my certification."

"How do you deal with it, the carnage and all?" Maggie slapped a mosquito that landed on her arm in bold defiance of Larkin's trap.

"The camera gives me a degree of separation between the carnage and myself. For an antidote, I counteract the gruesome with the awesome. First off, I am a nature and art portrait photographer." He patted the hard-shell camera case at his feet. "Don't go anywhere without it."

She recalled the initials scrawled on the picture hanging above the fireplace. "Is the elegant eagle picture in the Lake Room yours?"

"Thank you, yes. It was my house-warming gift. I shot that photo in Ketchikan, Alaska. When you've got an eagle zoomed up close and personal in your viewfinder and he's looking straight at you, you hope you're too large to be his lunch. Eagles there are like seagulls are to us here. There are hundreds of them on that small island."

"A majesty of eagles, wow!"

"Is that what a group of them is called?"

"I just now made it up, but I think the word is appropriate. Majestic, but they are fearsome."

"I'll give you that," he agreed, opening the cooler.

After *le soleil* tucked himself into bed, the fireworks would start. CJ said he hoped to capture the best pictures ever. For the moment, however, he allowed that he was quite content to be sitting beside the prettiest girl at the party, which made Maggie laugh.

Maggie caught herself mid-laugh and pondered. *Why, I have laughed more often since landing on brown soil than I ever did living on red dirt!*

CJ interrupted her thoughts. "Want one?" He reached into the cooler for a beer.

"I'll take a root beer, thank you, please. It feels good to sit a spell, away from the din and demands."

The warm night brought the heady smell of pine trees mingling with the distant smoke of the cookers burning off the meat drippings.

Shaking ice chunks off the can, he popped the tab and handed it to her.

"Did you take pictures of Bob Morgan at the scene?" She held the wet and dripping can away from her bare feet. As usual, her sandals were parked under the bench, minus her feet. She wiped the side of the can on the lower leg of her jeans then took a deep drink. Pulling her feet up, she sat cross-legged on the cedar bench.

"Yes, I did."

"Are you state appointed or free-lance?"

"I assist the sheriff. We're good friends. I help him whenever he needs me. I'm second on the call list for the Maine State Police."

"Do you have real job, or what?" Maggie was in full journalistic mode with her style of questions.

He laughed. "I'm a semi-retired rancher and horse trainer, and a professional photographer. Sadly, there's always a need for the forensic aspect. I take time out for artistic photography shoots. Like tonight."

He set his beer bottle on the ground beside the bench. Hunkering down on one knee, he removed the camera from the case.

Maggie thought the fire-emblazoned sun sliding downward in its journey toward Japan looked promising.

CJ fixed the camera on a sturdy tripod and adjusted its legs. After aiming it in the direction of the sun's expected journey, he fiddled with finite adjustments. Looking quite satisfied, he sat down. "Digital has gone pretty fancy. I programmed it for one frame per minute for sunset shots. Now we'll just wait for Nature to do her best."

The wind blew a kiss across the lake. Maggie pulled the shawl close around her shoulders.

"Should be seventy degrees now, according to the earlier prediction, but I don't believe it's anywhere close to that," she fussed. "In my not-so-humble opinion, if the weather people looked out a window occasionally, the forecast would be far more accurate." She tucked her hands under her thighs.

"Cold?" CJ slid closer and draped his arm around her shoulders. "Do you mind?"

"Not at all. Um, what does 'CJ' stand for?"

"The Pledge of Allegiance, a lady…"

Maggie poked him in the ribs. "Be serious!"

"Umpf! All right already! It's Colin Jesse. Colin Jesse Dubois."

"That's quite a combination of Irish, Hebrew, and French. Anything else?"

"English and American Indian are thrown in the immediate genetic woodpile, I'm told. I was called 'Colin' when I got into trouble. 'CJ' is friendlier and everyone can spell it."

"Anymore, that's too true," she said. "Kids nowadays don't read much or seem to learn to spell like they did in my school years. They've grown up watching TV and playing video games."

"I agree with you." CJ patted her shoulder in time with the toe-tapping country tune floating across the night air. "Television can be blamed for any number of things. Turning it on, you let people invade your living room that you would never invite to your house to begin with."

"There's a lot of truth to that." Maggie climbed onto her metaphoric soapbox. "I believe that TV has helped to corrupt the English language. It has reduced vocabulary to a first-grade level, and mocked ethics. The networks say that the public *wants* this trash because it raises the viewers' dopamine levels."

"What's dopamine?"

"Dopamine occurs naturally in our bodies, and is highly addictive. Ever notice how lethargic you are after watching TV for a while? Has anyone caught on that the first part of the word 'dopamine' is 'dope' and the second part is 'mine'?"

"The irony has escaped them," CJ answered. "I hadn't caught it either."

Maggie was still on her soapbox. "Don't you find sitcoms insulting? If anyone were to speak to me like some of those characters do, I'd spit 'em out in the middle of next week!"

"I have noticed," he said, taking a swig of beer.

"You what? When?" she yelped, perplexed. "What I said tonight to Victor Turner?"

"That, and after Morgan's funeral."

Maggie frowned and CJ laughed.

"Walker and I were off to the side. We watched the whole show with you and Turner. You were giving that ol' boy what-for and boy-howdy. I wouldn't want to have been in his shoes."

She blew out an upward breath, ruffling her bangs, and took a drink of her root beer. "He startled me. What he said put my back up," she said with a dignified sniff. She uncrossed her legs, stood up and stretched.

"He hadn't said more than a dozen words when you took aim. What set you off?"

Maggie ran both hands down her cheeks as if brushing away cobwebs. She turned to face him. "He accused me of deliberately insinuating myself into my uncle's good graces.

Going for the main chance. Not that he has any room to talk."

Seagulls called to one another in the distance, turning cartwheels in the darkening sky, dancing toward their nests, likely somewhere up on the craggy face of Old Man Mountain.

"What's he to you, that he'd say that? He kin to you?"

"I don't admit it out loud, but he's a cousin."

"Which side of the family?"

"Maternal. June, Victor's mother, is Rod's older sister. She has a mercenary streak in her, same as her sister Marion did." Her voice grew bitter with the recall. "Marion, my ostensible mother, who refined the mercenary attitude ..."

She broke off and sat down beside him. "I'm sorry, CJ. I'll hop off my soapbox now."

She stared at the cottage across the lake. Light was streaming like liquid sunshine from open windows, backlighting the people sitting on the porch. Kids played hopscotch and tag, their happy squeals carrying faintly across the water.

"You are a very opinionated woman," he said. "You seem to have a strong sense of black and white. There's very little gray in your world."

Maggie bristled, then calmed down. "Quite so. Doesn't leave much room for negotiation or compromise, does it?" At her feet, specks of dirt peeked through the trampled blades of grass like a shy child wanting to play.

"Not really. I'd better stay on your good side," he said with a quirky grin.

"So far, so good," she replied. She leaned against his arm

and snuggled a little closer.

"How much do you know about Turner, the adult version?" he asked, putting his empty beer bottle into a plastic bag looped on the arm of the bench. "Want another one?"

"Yes, thank you, please." She sat up to exchange her empty can for a fresh one. "Other than him likely on the make for ex-wife number fill-in-the-blank, not much. Right twistical, morally speaking."

"Sounds like he really believes in marriage – at least the concept of it." Turning sober, he said, "I'd urge you to stay as far away from him as you can."

"I'm not afraid of little Vicky. I'm bigger than he is, for starters."

"True, but he's got real mob connections, Maggie."

"Was that tall linebacker dude his bodyguard, maybe? He might be someone to stay away from. Since he was laughing about my dust-up with Victor, maybe he's tame."

CJ looked doubtful but remained quiet for the space of several minutes.

"Walker was wondering what he's doing here in the first place. In spite of their age difference, Turner and Morgan have had some shady business dealings in the past. But that's not enough reason for him to attend the funeral."

"Don't killers attend their victims' funerals?"

"They often do. Along with the police."

"Well, even considering his smarmy accusations, I don't really think he was checking up on *me*. Whyever for? We haven't seen each other for donkey's years. Perhaps he's a ghoul in disguise, and the funeral setting made him feel at home."

The gentle sounds of the pine trees whispering love songs to one another calmed Maggie but brought home to her just how much she had missed this simple joy.

Once again, she had the feeling that she'd known CJ somewhere in time or in some other place. He seemed so familiar, and she was comfortable with him almost from the first hello, which was unusual. She kept new male acquaintances at full arm's length until she could assess their temperaments and agendas.

Dampened by distance, filtered through firs, the strains of a song concerning the exploits of a frog named Jeremiah flitted across on the light breeze. Maggie patted her leg in time to the music.

"Will you go to the dance with me this Friday night?"

"What dance?" Maggie asked, still keeping time.

"At the Rusty Anchor. It's a little nicer than most bars."

She pulled one foot up onto the seat and rubbed her toes. "How's the floor?"

"It's a large dance floor, all wood." Nodding at her foot action, he added, "Clean, not sticky."

"That's encouraging. How's the music?"

"Country, soft rock. The Clipper Ship Band is the house band. They've been playing here all day. Who didn't you dance with tonight? Got boots?"

"Of course I have boots, silly, and I prefer dancing country. Ballroom's all right, on occasion."

She thought for a moment, picturing her aunt's busy social calendar. "Oops, not this Friday, I'm sorry. Larkin and I are going to the Quilt Society meeting. I'd be pleased to go with you on Saturday night instead, if that's an option." On impulse, she leaned over and gave him a quick kiss on the cheek.

After a short pause, he said, "It is. Great. I'm looking forward to it."

"Me, too. Thank you. Um, tomorrow afternoon, maybe you would take me to look at the crime scene? Where Bob Morgan was murdered, I mean. That is, if the crime scene tape is down? Please?"

"Whoa, Maggie! Who said it was murder?"

At the shoreline, very close to where they were sitting, a loon cried out and his mate answered. Bird song and water lapping the rocky shore were nature's counterpoint for humankind's music filtering through the trees.

"Well, isn't it murder? New in town and even *I* am hearing the rustling leaves of Birdie's news-vine. Weren't too many who liked Bob Morgan. One person might have clicked that dislike up a notch or two."

A brilliant red-orange blaze creating a fiery halo, its embers forging an imprint of the sun on the horizon, caught their attention. CJ jumped up and peered through the camera's viewfinder.

"I'll check with Walker first." He pushed a button on the camera, watched the display for a full minute then sat back down.

"Do you like digital?"

"It took me a while to get used to it. I do like it better," he answered. "No more advancing the film after each shot. No stopping to reload right in the middle of a time-sensitive sequence. The review and edit is wonderful. It's the wave of the future."

"Quite so. I'll stick to my Minolta SLR for now," Maggie replied, shifting on the hard bench seat. "I'm not going to switch over until the last roll of film is ancient history."

"Back to your earlier question, Maggie. Why in thunderation do you want to see the site of an accident? Where a man died?"

CJ stood, linked his hands together and reached high over his head, slapping a pine tree limb as he stretched. The sunset was fading into nothingness. He unfolded, and then leaned over to stop the camera's action.

She took a drink of her root beer before answering. "Curiosity."

Snatches of a tune asking someone to take something to the limit one more time filtered across the night air. Maggie wished she were on the dance floor with … *With whom?*

CJ sat down. "My old Gran would have called it spunky," he said in a low undertone.

"What time tomorrow? What time Saturday? Rod said I can use his Jeep, but I would rather you picked me up."

Answering in reverse order of her rapid-fire questions, CJ said, "Of course I'll pick you up, right at the front door Saturday, say about five? We can go out for dinner. The band starts playing at eight. About tomorrow, I'll call you after I talk to the sheriff."

"Oh, he shouldn't object," she said, full of confidence. She started rubbing her back against the bench, back and forth. CJ pushed her forward and scratched her back all over.

"Up, up a bit. Thanks. Doggon skeeters! Don't think this

sugar-water gizmo works."

"Seems to have helped some. Ordinarily there's a whole platoon of the pesky buggers out at this time of night."

Addressing his previous question, she said, "Why do I want to go there? How else can I write 'The Best Mystery Story Ever' if I don't have a first-hand chance at real sleuthing? Besides, I often wonder how contrived most mystery book plots really are. And I'd like to find out whether I am more observant than some of those fictional protagonists."

She flashed back to the bank robbery. She was thankful that she'd been out of the front lobby at the time, but she still remembered the deafening blast of the gunshots with absolute clarity: horribly devastating, terrifying in their finality. She had vamoosed out of Dodge/Tucson, with nary a backward glance.

Locking that horror back in the dank attic from whence it had escaped, she said, apropos to nothing, "Only ten days remain before I leave for Oklahoma." She sang along with the band's signature good-night-sweetheart song: *"Wish you didn't have to go ..."*

The final chords were fading out when, out of the corner of her eye, Maggie thought she saw a deep shadow move near the trees. She turned in her seat and caught a glimpse of a person standing within earshot. Man or woman? She couldn't tell, the darkness morphing the person into an ambiguous shape. With hundreds of people wandering around tonight, there were bound to be others wanting to share this vantage spot, so she thought nothing more about it.

"It's almost dark enough. The fireworks should start

soon." CJ leaned toward the camera and upped the frame sequence timing for fast action. "Now!"

The fireworks blossomed in brimstone brilliance against the backdrop of the velvety sky. Boom! Pop! Sizzle! Starbursts fit to make the rainbow envious. The sounds drowned out the chance of further conversation and covered up the snapping of twigs.

15

Maggie Finds a Clue

Thursday, July 5ᵗʰ, early afternoon

"**WHAT'RE YOU DRIVING AT, CJ?**" Sheriff Walker Bainbridge climbed out of his patrol car. "And just what do you think *you're* doing, Maggie?"

CJ stood beside Maggie with his arms crossed. He put one hand up to hide his grin.

"You gave us permission, remember? Don't huff, Sheriff. I'm a writer and I notice things. Goes with the territory." She brushed back a strand of hair escaping the pins that were falling down on the job.

"Amateur sleuthing can be hazardous to your health if you're not careful," he replied.

Maggie kicked the gravel with the toe of her boot.

"This isn't a book, Maggie."

She scowled at him and gritted her teeth.

CJ uncrossed his arms. "Seriously, Walker, you'll be interested in what we found. Morgan's death looks more like murder than an accident. You'll need to see this before the truck is taken off to parts unknown."

"In my considered opinion, Sheriff, Bob Morgan didn't just trip over himself and die. He was helped. Murdered, that is." Maggie turned on her boot heel and headed for Morgan's truck.

"When I am ready to consider your opinion, I'll let you know," he answered, following one step behind her. "Civilians," he muttered. "All right, show me what you two found."

Before CJ could reply, Maggie jumped in. "Several things. There's a dent on the hood, near the nose. And some scratches right there." She pointed to the faint ragged marks in the paint near the windshield, and the slight gouge further down on the hood.

The sheriff grabbed her hand.

"I'm not touching, just pointing!"

After looking at the marks, he said, "So? What're a few scratches? Maybe a squirrel took a nosedive out of the tree, landed hard, and scratched the paint."

Maggie shot him a get-outta-town look. The sheriff chuckled.

"Morgan was fanatical about his truck. Loose with women, free with booze, but his truck was a whole 'nother story. It's a known fact that a dent wouldn't have time to settle before he'd have it fixed."

She was grateful that CJ had entered the fray before it escalated.

"He didn't drive all week. My people were on patrol and made sure he didn't. Though it would have pleased me to no end to have locked him up on a DUI."

"If Bob Morgan was wearing a belt and he slid or rolled off the hood, his buckle would make scratches, right?" Maggie asked in a reasonable tone, hoping he would agree.

"Might have," Sheriff Bainbridge conceded. He walked

to the front of the truck with Maggie dogging his heels.

"And falling from that distance, the momentum carrying him forward," she hesitated, "well, that extra force behind him when he hit the rocks ..." Her voice faded in spite of her earlier enthusiasm. She felt a bit pale around the gills.

"What extra force?" the sheriff barked. He took a small notebook and pen out of his uniform pocket.

His sharp question helped Maggie refocus. She crossed her arms behind her back, tucking her hands palm outward in the back pockets of her faded jeans. "Okay. Since it's been parked here without anyone driving it meanwhile ..." She pulled out her left hand and pointed. "He was found right here, right? A short distance away from the front of the truck?"

Both men bobbed their heads in agreement. She removed her other hand and knelt down on one knee near the left rear tire.

"See how the gravel has been kicked up here, in front of the tire? Like the truck had been parked there a while before it was backed up with force. There's too much dirt showing right here, where gravel should be."

"Here, let me at it." The sheriff put out his big paw to help her up. He bent down closer. "CJ, get your camera."

"One more thing, Sheriff," Maggie said. "The driver's side door isn't shut all the way."

He peered at the tiny gap between the door and the frame. "Huh, you're right. It's been eased shut. Tight enough to kick the interior light off, though. Good catch, Maggie."

"The other odd thing, Walker," CJ said, removing his camera from its case, "Morgan always bragged about leaving his keys in the ignition. They aren't there now."

"Maybe his wife has them. I want to talk to her again anyway."

Maggie handed a small white object to the sheriff. "And I found this."

"What is it?"

"It's a pearl, Sheriff."

"I know that, Maggie. My wife loves pearls."

"It's half-drilled and would be mounted on an up-eye or a post. Used for a necklace drop, earrings, or a tie stud." At his questioning look, she added, "I make jewelry, too, and I know about these things."

"And just where did you find it?" He crossed his beefy arms across his wide chest.

"Maggie spotted it on the ground, close to where the body was found," CJ interjected. He reviewed the images on the camera's display screen. "She picked it up before I knew what she was after."

"According to your uncle you read enough mysteries, so you should know better. You're not supposed to touch or pick up anything at a crime scene."

"Crime scene? Then you agree it *was* murder?" Gratified, she ignored his scolding.

"Maybe," he allowed. He went to his patrol car and returned with a small plastic bag. He dropped the pearl into it. "This may be evidence."

"Don't glare at me, Sheriff. I am aware of the need to preserve evidence, but I love beads. I'm sorry."

"Fingerprints, Maggie!" he exploded. "Yours are on this pearl."

"Well, yours are on it now, too. Besides, it's too small to pick up any." *I hope.*

Sticking her tongue out at the sheriff was not politic, not to mention being quite childish and wholly unbefitting a fifty-something woman. Maggie forbore to do so even though she engaged with great satisfaction in the mental imagery.

"CJ! Get her out of here." He reached for his left-side holster.

Maggie swallowed a breath and quick-stepped back.

The sheriff whipped out his cell phone. "I'm calling an impound wrecker and the State Police. CJ, I'll meet up with you later."

Maggie noticed that CJ was having a difficult time keeping a straight face. She glowered at him, and he burst out laughing.

Taking her by the elbow, still chuckling, CJ led her to the passenger door of his truck. "Come on, Miss Maggie, let's go for a ride. The sooner we are out of Walker's way the happier we will all be."

"I hope he's not too angry with me. I'd like to think he's pleased with what we found."

"The sheriff and his department are a crackerjack team, Maggie. They are fully trained officers, professional, savvy, and educated. Don't ever underestimate him or his crew." He helped her navigate the double steps up into the cab of the truck.

"I know that, CJ. Bumbling idiots on the police force don't make it very far, regardless how some writers portray them."

Buckling up, he started the engine. "You had beginner's luck. You found several things the initial team missed, which is unusual for them." He released the parking brake. "I'm glad you didn't stick your tongue out at him. I don't think I could go your bail."

"What!" Maggie felt the heat rise past her eyebrows. "I did *not* stick my tongue ... how could you even *think* that?" She clicked her seatbelt in place.

"Your face, Miss Maggie. You should never play poker."

16

Maggie Travels the Dusty Backstreets of Memory

Thursday, July 5ᵗʰ, afternoon

"**WOULD YOU MIND, CJ,** going for an old-fashioned drive? Maybe go to Augusta and out Western Avenue? Or down to Hallowell? Seems like I've been away a hundred years."

"Maggie, Miss Dixie and I will be happy to take you for a Sunday drive."

Miss Dixie: This year's model truck, elegant in silver-gray satin, the color of a dove's wing in moonlight. From the first time she saw it a few hours ago when CJ picked her up at Eagles' Rest, Maggie had liked the truck.

"Even on Thursday?"

"Even on Thursday."

"Then maybe later, have ice cream instead of dinner, or do I mean supper?"

"Yankees call the noon meal 'dinner,' and the evening meal is 'supper.' The lunch break is called 'nooning,' but lunch goes in your dinner bucket, if you aren't confused enough already." CJ signaled for a left turn onto Morrilton Road.

"Beyond confused. How about 'let's just go eat' later?"

"That'll work. Want some music?"

"Sure. Soft rock, oldies, or country? What station?"

"Not the radio. Under your seat there's a case of CDs. You choose."

Maggie flipped through the selections: Rod Stewart, Bob Dylan, Charlie Rich, Pete Seeger, Odetta, Emmy Lou Harris, Clint Black, Righteous Brothers, The Mamas and Papas, Reba, Dwight Yoakam, and more. It was a very eclectic mix.

Soft refrains, talk-to-your-heart kind of music, that's the ticket. She slipped a disc into the player. Emmy Lou's evocative melodies blended in a haunting, soft counterpoint to the steady hum of the truck's engine. Maggie leaned back in her seat, closed her eyes, and let the music drift over her psychic weariness.

Miss Dixie took them faithfully up hill, down dale, traveling today's highways while trekking down the intangible, fickle paths of Memory Lane.

Maggie had graduated from Hall-Dale High School in Farmingdale at the age of seventeen. She was a few days older than the baby of the class. Then she remembered that the youngest classmate had died in a tragic accident a long time ago, thereby making Maggie the youngest of her class by default.

"Even with the press of time, some things never change." They drove by the school's campus. "Except everything looks so small now."

Other than an occasional comment about a house or landmark, or absence thereof, Maggie didn't say much during the long drive going nowhere and everywhere. In Hallowell, at her request, CJ drove down Park Street. The old house didn't look like it had changed very much in the decades since she'd last seen it.

The yellow glow of incandescent lights feathered the edges of the drawn shades, indicating that Aunt June was home. However, Maggie had no intention of knocking on her door, ever. The elegant Lexus parked in the driveway lent an incongruous note to the shabby old house. Maggie doubted that it was penny-pinching Aunt June's car. Maybe Victor, spoiled brat that he still was, even in his early sixties, was visiting his mother?

At the bottom of the steep hill that was Park Street, CJ turned left onto State Street, the road running parallel to the Kennebec River.

"How about stopping for that ice cream? You must be hungry by now, Maggie. I am."

"Dairy Queen?" she asked, perking up.

"You got it."

17

Maggie Wades through Sticky Thickets

Thursday, July 5ᵗʰ, late evening

SURVEYING THE INADEQUATE PAPER NAPKIN adhering with singular determination to his caramel-sticky fingers, CJ looked across the table at Maggie. "This is not working. I'll be right back."

Maggie, already having divested herself of things gooey, toyed with the soggy napkin stuck under her water glass. Her mind was going in six different directions, all at the same time.

CJ returned and sat down beside her. "Maggie, what's fretting you?" he asked, keeping his voice low. There were several groups of people scattered about the dining area. Some were quiet and others anything but, like the four teenagers cutting up at the far table.

She picked up her glass, peeled off the napkin, and took a long drink of water. "Gypsy wind."

She felt him stiffen for a moment. He put his right arm along the back of her seat with his hand brushing her shoulder. *Could get used to this,* she thought.

He moved a lock of stray hair away from her face. "Explain, please."

"It's my catch-phrase: gypsy wind. My feeble attempt to

describe a strange mood that comes over me at odd times –
an echo, a restlessness of mind, or uneasiness in my spirit.
Sometimes a song triggers it. Certain weather. It's like not
knowing whether to stand or run, so I do neither."

Dr. Vickie was right, Maggie conceded. *I did need this
vacation.*

Sighing, she looked up at CJ. Heavy streaks of silver ran
through his thick, dark brown hair. An indentation around his
crown showed a hat line. There were a few creases and
wrinkles in his square face, a nice face. Over all, he was
looking pretty good for a guy maybe cruising on the near
starboard side of sixty years old.

He smiled at her and patted her shoulder.

Cute dimple when he smiles.

"How old are you?" Maggie asked.

"I'll be sixty-one next month. You?"

"I'm fifty-seven."

"I thought a lady never told her age." The crinkles
around his brown eyes deepened with his teasing.

"Doesn't bother me. The person looking back at me in
the mirror is not the person I am inside."

"What year did you graduate?"

Maggie wondered what it mattered in the grand scheme
of things, but answered anyway. "In 1967."

The noisy young foursome made their rowdy way to the
front door, joking and jostling each other around. The
manager walked up and chided them. The teenagers stopped
their shenanigans and left the premises without further
incident.

"Rod mentioned that you are here on a medical leave of

absence. What happened, if I'm not prying into something I shouldn't?"

"You're not. My best friend is a doctor. Vickie recognized that I needed a serious respite from all the heavy stuff that has come my way in the last few years."

He cocked one brow upward in an unspoken question.

In a soft undertone, she gave him the bullet-point version of those psyche-battering events. CJ did not interrupt. He simply held her closer when she skimmed over the bank robbery.

"Anyway, Dr. Vickie was very insistent. She wrote out the professional order that allowed me to take time off without losing any personal vacation time, or forfeit my job. It isn't in my psychic makeup to have a nervous breakdown. The leave was ordered so I could think, plan, and reassess my life. Decide where I want to be, what I want to do." *When I grow up? Really? Whatcha gonna do, Maggie Storm Blue?*

"Maggie." CJ paused and rubbed his hand over his face. "Some of the things you say and do, well … "

Maggie remained quiet, waiting for CJ to elaborate.

"Many of the places we went by today brought back memories for me, too."

"Déjà vu?" she asked, tilting her head, looking up at him.

He lifted his shoulders in a noncommittal shrug. "Could be."

"Right weird feeling, that."

"I agree."

Sensing that her emotional boat was rocking though she could not have said why, she was headed for calmer waters when CJ spoke up.

"You're about as American as they come. But you use a lot of British expressions and word patterns. So where'd you pick that up?"

She gave him a sheepish lopsided grin. "Blame Mary in payroll. She was born in England, married an American, and came to Oklahoma City twenty years ago. We go to lunch at least twice a week, so I've picked up a lot from her. Also, many of the cozy mysteries I love are set in England."

"You're a chameleon, then."

"Or a parrot. When I go back to work, I'll be teased about regaining my Downeast accent."

An older couple at the adjoining table picked up the detritus of their meal. After they were gone, the place was almost empty. A few customers were at the front counter ordering take-out. Since it was a Thursday night, the Dairy Queen was quieter than if it were a weekend night.

Pursuing the reason they had scattered out of the sheriff's way earlier, Maggie said, "Look at this business with Bob Morgan, for instance."

"You're changing subjects again."

"No, I'm not." She hesitated for a tick. "Well, yes, I am. He was murdered, CJ, I just know it."

"I won't argue about that. Not after what you showed us today."

"What about Walker? Has he called to tell you anything? Does he really believe us that it was murder?" she asked, her earlier melancholic mood forgotten.

He unclipped his cell phone. "We've been together, hardly out of each other's sight, for the last eight hours." He glanced at the phone. "Nine hours. No messages. He doesn't share all of his cases with me either, you know. And he's not going to share much with you, unless it suits him to, for his benefit, or your safety." He shut the phone and clipped it onto his belt.

She leaned back. "Calling it an accident doesn't make sense, at least not to me. The kicked-up gravel and the scratches on the hood both point to murder."

"Either way, he's just as dead."

"The truck is the clue, or the method, whichever. So, if the scratches were made by his belt buckle, maybe he was up on the hood sleeping, or passed out."

"Why wouldn't he sleep in his own bed?" CJ reached for her glass and drank the rest of the water. "The house wasn't locked."

"Who knows how a drunk's thought processes work? Convenience? Waiting for someone?"

"Maybe the truck *was* moved, causing him to fall off. You pointed that out perfectly."

"Fingerprints are not over-rated. Surely the sheriff has a superb forensic team to go over that vehicle, doesn't he?"

"He does. They will go over it, Maggie. You can bet on it. Both his crew and the State Police are involved now. Your imagination, or intuition, is working overtime, but it is something to chew on."

Maggie shot him a look. No, he was not patronizing her. His deep brown eyes were thoughtful.

"Intuition, yes, but not in the feminine sense," she said. "Intuition is one of the Holy Spirit's ways of nudging one's consciousness into heightened awareness. There's a disparity of facts. Just haven't made sense of it. Yet."

"You may not have all the facts. Motive is one piece that's missing. Method is another," CJ reminded her.

"I just gave you one scenario for method."

"I mean the whole thing seems too unpredictable. Unplanned."

"Right chancy, that. Who could have known Morgan would be there at that precise moment, or how drunk he would be? That's far too random for the whim of chance and circumstance to play that card successfully. Unless the murderer was stalking him, waiting for a window of opportunity for an ambush. That makes it either premeditation or perfect timing. Perhaps not intending to kill him, only to scare the bewhalers out of him."

"So, the murderer took whatever was handy for the means, which turned fatal."

"If Morgan was asleep on the hood, the murderer would have to think up a plan in a big hurry as to how she was going to kill him. And then act wicked fast before he woke up and objected to playing the starring role," she reasoned.

"*She*? Are you going feminist with your pronouns?"

"Not quite, though seriously, I think this is too tidy for a man to have done it. That's not a feminist remark but an observation. Doing the deed long-distance, one step removed, is neater. I think a man would have beaten the stuffing out of Morgan, or something worse. Just a hunch."

"What about someone like Victor Turner? He might not want to dirty his hands either. Morgan was six-foot tall. I don't think Turner, with his small frame, would tangle with him. Long-distance would suit him, too."

"There is that," Maggie agreed. She wouldn't mind one little bit seeing her obnoxious cousin behind bars.

"Which brings us back to motive."

"Motive just means why. That's easy. Bob's a batterer and probably an adulterer, and who knows what else he got up to? Disgruntled customer? Maybe even a spot of blackmail? Half the town didn't cry when he died, and the other half rejoiced."

"Yes, even you, Maggie, were heard to say you'd be a widow if you were married to the likes of him." He picked up his hat and put it on.

"Well, I am not his widow, so that lets me out. Besides, I have never even met the man."

"It's no secret that you've no use for his kind," he said, his gaze remaining fixed on her face.

Maggie conceded his point. "True. But that does not mean I would turn right vigilantical and dispense justice outside of the law."

CJ dropped his intent stare. "Is 'vigilantical' a real word?"

"No, but it should be. It's a vigilante with a kick-butt attitude."

CJ chuckled and glanced at his watch. "It's going on nine. Are you ready, Miss Maggie? Miss Dixie is waiting for us. And the Richardsons, too, I'll bet, are waiting on you." He stood up and held out his hand.

"They know I'm with you, CJ. Thanks for the compliment, but I'm long gone from needing a curfew." She picked up her purse and reached for his hand.

He pulled her close to him, looking in her eyes for a long

minute as though he was peering past the years. They went out, her hand tucked in the crook of his arm.

"Why did you name your truck 'Miss Dixie'?" she asked after he helped her up the steps and seated her.

"A Texas kind of thinking." He buckled up and started the engine. "Did you know that the State constitution reserves the right for Texans to withdraw their statehood from the Union if they ever felt they had sufficient reason to do so?"

"Truth?"

"Truth. I like that independent spirit and the Texas state of mind."

"CJ? I've spent many years in the South. A lot of your mannerisms and speech patterns, well, they are pure Texas. Yet you're real easy with Yankee speak. What gives?"

"Miss Maggie," he drawled. She laughed, and he said, "You're right on target. Most of my younger grade school years were spent in a small town near Portland. I joined the Marines right after graduating from high school. After my stint in 'Nam I went to college. I stayed in California for about a year afterward. Then I came back here for a very short time."

"Why didn't you stay here?"

"My reason to stay had disappeared."

She sat very still, staring out the windshield, lost in thought.

After a few miles, CJ broke the silence. "I was away too long. When I came home, it was too late. You can't hold a wanderer. She was gone, and I let her go. Later, I regretted that decision. A few years ago, I searched for my long-ago sweetheart. I didn't find her."

Maggie bowed her head and toyed with her rings. "Oh." She didn't like love stories with sad endings.

CJ was quiet over the space of several minutes. "Photography took me many places, all over the world, in fact. In my travels, I met a lady who had a working horse ranch, the Rockin' Diamond D, in the green country of northeast Texas, in Franklin County. We were married and had the requisite two-point-seven children."

He turned off Morrilton Road onto Franklin Road and traveled at a sedate speed along the main street of Baysinger Cove.

After being on the state highway, Maggie felt like they were crawling.

"Two point seven?"

"Two kids, and Point Seven is what Ann named the dog."

"Ann – your wife?"

"Yes. Ann died from complications of pneumonia. I moved here about ten years ago."

"So, any reason to return to Texas?"

"No reason to move back, if that's what you mean. He insisted on buying it, so I sold the ranch itself to our son, Chase. He and his family live there now. I still own a major share of our horse business, so I visit periodically. Our daughter, Michaela, is a lawyer. She lives with her family in Oregon."

"Have you any other family?"

After a short silence, he said, "None."

Maggie suspected the one-word answer meant the subject

was closed. "So, now you're here."

"Now I'm here."

He coasted around the circular driveway of Eagles' Rest and turned off the engine.

"And now you're home."

I wish, Maggie prayed as he helped her descend the truck's steep steps.

"Thank you, CJ, for taking me all over everywhere tonight and being so patient. For telling me a bit more about yourself and listening to my tale of misery. Some things are real hard to talk about with a stranger—"

"You don't feel much like a stranger to me," he interrupted. They walked, her arm tucked in his, along the path around to the staircase leading up to the balcony deck of the guest quarters.

She halted and snugged his arm tighter.

He froze. "What?"

"Nothing. Well, I heard twigs snapping."

"City girl, you're in the country now. Twigs snap for good reason. Night critters have to eat too."

"Oh!"

With her slender hand in his large one, they climbed the staircase to the screened-in upper deck. The outer screen door wasn't locked; it had no need to be. CJ brushed a kiss across her lips, hesitated, then kissed her again, good and proper.

A little dizzy from the unexpected kiss, she reached in her crazy-quilted purse and unclipped her key from its mooring. It slipped out of her hand and dropped on the floor. CJ picked it up, unlocked the door to the guest suite and returned her key. Maggie placed her hand lightly against his chest and kissed him back.

"Good night, Miss Maggie. Now scoot! It's late."

With a cat-who-ate-the-canary smile, she stepped across the threshold into the suite, easing the door closed behind her.

18

Maggie Finds a Lull in the Storm?

Friday, July 6th, morning

"**MORNIN'.**" **MAGGIE YAWNED,** rubbed her eyes and blinked twice in a blurry attempt to focus on the cobalt blue glass coffee mug parked beside the coffee carafe. Her eyeglasses were still upstairs on the nightstand. She would have to view the world through optical assist soon enough. Now, however, soft focus was the finest kind.

She poured a steaming cup of the heavenly-smelling coffee. Sipping cautiously, she breathed in the aromatic vapors bathing her face. Addicted to morning coffee, she was − a tame addiction by anyone's standards.

"Ahh, Creole, isn't it? Good stuff. Wakes you right up, whether you want to be, or not. Yeowser!" She sat down in the breakfast room with her back to the window, basking in the early morning sun.

"Mornin' to you, sleepyhead. Yes, dear, it is Creole coffee." Larkin brushed toast crumbs off her napkin onto her plate. "No one around here carries it, so I have to order it."

Rod snapped his newspaper open. "We get a case at a time. That way we won't run out in a hurry."

"How are you? Did you sleep well?" Larkin asked.

"Sleep? Uh-hum." Maggie took another sip of coffee.

Elegant. Elegant, huh? Finest kind? I'm drifting back into Yankee-speak real easy this morning. "What time is it?"

"It's seven-thirty, dear."

"Good. Plenty of time left to wake up. I was reading a Mary Jane Clark mystery and couldn't put it down until the wee hours." Maggie gave her aunt a loving smile. "You're spoiling me."

"Glad to do it," Larkin answered. "We all need pampering from time to time."

Maggie admitted that she did not have a willing handshake agreement with mornings. However, after an infusion of coffee, she could, and would, function when it was needful to do so. "An owl, oh, yes. A lark? Only under duress," she informed her relatives.

She went out to the kitchen for a coffee refill then stood at the end of the kitchen island nearest the breakfast room. From this vantage point, Maggie caught her own reflection in the full-length mirror on the utility room door. The dark blue silk caftan was perfect for her tall, still slim figure. Her hair was sleep tussled, the long, fine strands glowing like a dusky raven's wing in the morning light.

Rod jerked and dropped the newspaper. Turning toward his wife, he said in a low, shaky voice, "She ... Ma—"

Interrupting him, Larkin grabbed his arm. "Darlin', are you all right? You're as pale as a ghost." Worry colored her drawl.

"Um, yes. A ghost just walked across my grave." He hunched up his shoulders as if he were cold.

"Don't you mean 'goose,' dear?" she asked with all the assurance of a woman who knows she's right.

"No, Larkin, my literary wizard, not this time. Definitely a ghost." He picked up his paper and resumed reading.

Maggie glided into the breakfast room. Sitting down in the wicker chair, she glanced at her uncle. The slight tremor of the newspaper pages was the only outward sign that something had shaken him. His eyebrows nearly met in the middle, causing extra-deep creases above his nose, and his jade-green eyes looked pensive. *Too early for drama of any sort,* she decided, and let her uncle's strange, disjointed comment go.

Sheba seemed glad to have her new human friend downstairs. The dog plopped down with a soft paw resting on Maggie's bare left foot. Cooing sweet nothings, she scratched the downy-soft ears and furry chin.

Larkin went to the kitchen to put raisin bread in the toaster. A few moments later, the toast popped up. Using bamboo tongs, Larkin dropped the hot slices onto two bread plates then returned to the breakfast room. She passed one plate to Maggie.

"Dear, what did you do after visiting the Morgan place yesterday?" she asked Maggie, curiosity shining in her bright blue eyes. "Walker said you'd unearthed some good information before he chased you out."

Maggie thanked her and asked, "When did you see him?"

"Walker drops by most mornings for early coffee. Rod's usually up at the crack of dawn. I'm not quite that chipper. Seven's more to my liking." Larkin moved the butter dish closer to her niece.

Maggie slathered her toast with the real creamery butter. "I don't blame him for being miffed and chasing us out.

Afterward, CJ drove for hours, bless his patient little socks. He indulged my whim to take a trip up and down Memory Lane. We went all over Hallowell, Farmingdale, and Augusta. The only place we closed down was the Dairy Queen. That's how rowdy a pair we are." Maggie set her mouth in a rueful smile then indulged in an early-morning yawn.

The raisin bread was bakery-made, toasted crispy, and simply melt-in-your-mouth delicious. Maggie wiped butter from her chin with a soft cloth napkin.

"He's a very nice man." Rod folded his paper. "So is Walker. Takes his job seriously."

"What do you know about him?" she asked, elbows on the table, both hands wrapped around the blue coffee mug.

"CJ, you mean?"

Following the affirmative nod from Maggie, Rod said, "He joined the Marines in the mid-sixties. Vietnam."

That single word evoked volumes of history and full-bore emotion.

"He's always been clever with a camera. He mustered out of the service and went to college in California. Graduated with a major in photography, both journalistic and artistic. Met his wife-to-be and then moved to Texas. Some time after he married, he became a certified forensic photographer. His wife was a very successful rancher. She raised thoroughbred horses and taught him the business. She died, oh, about twelve years back."

"Did he ever mention what schools he attended here in Maine, or his parents, or any siblings?"

"He's quite close to the vest on some things, Maggie.

When he's ready, he'll talk. I'm a good judge of character, m'dear, and of the few good men out there, CJ Dubois is one of them."

"If you like him, that's all I really need to know, Uncle," she said with sincerity. She walked over to the coffee carafe and returned with it, setting it on the quilted hot pad in the center of the glass-topped table.

"About ten years ago, he relocated to Baysinger Cove. It's interesting how so many Yankees do come home again."

Rod talked about their many years of travel and how, even by a circuitous route, he'd eventually found his way back home, too. "I'm grateful that you call this place home, Larkin, m'love," he added, patting his wife's hand.

"Darlin', my home is where you are," she affirmed. "Among other places, we even lived in New Mexico for a while. We didn't like it much. Rod retired from the Air Force and then took a job in Georgia. I co-owned an antiques store there with my sister. I sold my interest to her when Rod retired for the last time. Just like homing pigeons, we flew back. I was born and raised in Georgia, but I love living here."

Larkin leaned over for a quick kiss, which Rod returned with double interest.

"What's on the docket for today, ladies?"

"Tonight's the Quilt Society meeting. Maggie, do you still want to go?"

Maggie, her mouth full, nodded in affirmation.

"Well, then, I think a quiet at-home day is in order." Larkin glanced out the bay window. "Looks like it's comin' on a storm. We surely do need the rain. There's a good breeze coming off the lake. It will be nice in the North Room. We'll just stitch and chat all day. Didn't you just get the newest Carolyn Hart book from The Happy Bookworm? You could read while we ply needles to cloth. Or whatever you wish to do, darlin'."

"Good plan. An easy day, I can handle that. The crew that came yesterday thoroughly cleaned up the grounds. There's nothing much left for me to do. I'll canvass the area to make sure they didn't miss anything before I head over to CJ's this afternoon." He drank the rest of his coffee and picked up the folded newspaper. "I'll make us some grilled cheese sandwiches for lunch, if that sounds good."

Rod took his cup to the kitchen sink, rinsed it and put it in the dishwasher. Sheba wanted out. He tossed the newspaper in the recycle bin on his way to the north kitchen door, with the dog two steps ahead of him.

In the guest suite, Maggie went through the rituals to make herself presentable for pleasant pastimes. It took minor miracles and major cosmetics, anymore. She was well over fifty years old and dancing closer to the next decade. Yeowser! *One is only as old as one feels?* Today she felt every minute of her age. Mercy, she was tired, albeit a happy tired. Yesterday had been an emotional roller coaster ride. She thought she was far beyond acting like a heartsick teenager. *At my age, really!*

"Oh, Lord," she prayed. "Help me make the right choices. Guide me. I'm confused, totally bumfuzzled. Lock the doors you don't want me to walk through, and open wide the ones you do. Please."

19

Maggie Faces a Dilemma

Friday July 6ᵗʰ, mid-morning

"MIND IF I CHECK MY E-MAILS?" Maggie asked her uncle before he went down the stairs.

"Sure, go ahead. I've got some phone calls to make. Take your time."

Rod's den was upstairs at the southeast corner of the house. It was paneled with oak bead-board wainscoting. The wall above the chair rail was painted a dark hunter green. A masculine room yet very comfortable. The décor was Bob Timberlake meets Rod Richardson style.

His computer was a Macintosh, the latest one, with super-fast Internet service, too. Sitting in his comfortable chair at the massive oak desk, she signed on. Of the forty-five messages that had come in since she had checked her mail two days ago, only two were of immediate interest, and she deleted the remainder.

The neighbor who had agreed to watch her house sent an update:

> Everything's fine here but your pothos
> is dead.

"How can anyone kill a pothos?" she muttered. They were supposed to be indestructible, even with *her* brown thumb. Did her neighbor give it a decent burial, perchance?

She read further:

> It was a real goner so I tossed it in the dumpster.

That's a decent burial? She smiled and typed:

> Okay. Don't fret about a dumb plant. See you on Sunday the 15th. Please don't forget to pick me up at the airport! If anything changes, I'll call you. Thanks!

The second message was from her boss. Maggie considered deleting it but thought better of it, wondering what the ruckus was about *this* time.

> Maggie, you've got to come back NOW! It's really not Elbert's fault that the computer crashed yesterday! We're already way behind. What can we do? You MUST get the next flight out.

"Fat chance." Never mind that she had a doctor's signature on her leave of absence order. Right brassy of that woman to even ask! She gritted her teeth, composing her thoughts into something fit to print, maybe even keep her from recriminations, before answering. Annoyed, she clicked REPLY and began typing:

> Call the Computer Whiz Kid Company. Alvin can fix anything. What can YOU do? Purchase a second computer. TWO computers, if the wounded one is beyond resuscitation. Meanwhile, you could make Elbert work late and weekends to catch up on what he

screwed up. See you at 10 a.m. on
TUESDAY the 17th. Maggie

"And not one minute sooner," she vowed as she clicked SEND.

Elbert-Brat wouldn't appreciate having his busy little social calendar compromised. How high was the mound of garbage that would be waiting for her? Was taking this much time off, even under a doctor's orders to retreat, worth the added stress it created for the first week back at work? Eleven more days remained before she would be back in her office. Once there, she'd address that trash. "If I still have a job," she said to the non-responsive computer screen.

Defying the obvious directive to return before the thirty days expired, though Mrs. Allgood had no right to make the demand, might be the turning point − but for whom? For them or me? Oh, well, Lord, it's all up to you.

Maggie signed off and headed across the hall to join her aunt in the North Room. Dear, sweet Larkin, they don't make 'em like her anymore.

Whatcha gonna do, Maggie Storm Blue?

"I am going to enjoy every single minute of every one of these remaining days, thank you very much."

20

Maggie Hears Ring-Ding-Ding

Friday, July 6th, late afternoon

MAGGIE WAS TAKING HER CLOTHES out of the dryer when the phone rang.

"Hello, Richardson residence, Maggie speaking."

"You still here? When you gonna leave?" The man's tone was gruff and sounded like he was juggling marbles against his tonsils. "You ain't wanted here. GO HOME!"

"I'll go home when I'm good and ready. You tell that reprobate Victor that it's ..."

The dial tone told Maggie that her shot in the dark hit its target.

"Who was that, Maggie?" Rod came through the utility room into the kitchen, wiping the sweat off his forehead with a paper towel.

She set the phone back in its base and started pacing. "Oh, that squirmy little piss-ant! Too scared to make the call himself so he got his linebacker dude buddy to do it. I'm getting awfully tired of his threats and insinuations."

Rod chuckled as he dispensed ice and water from the refrigerator door. "Victor, you mean?"

"Yeah, him. He says I'm trying to insinuate myself into your good graces so I can be the Golden Girl."

"Meaning?" Rod's jade green eyes had shifted to dark green.

"Finagling around, influencing you so I will inherit everything, and cutting Victor and my sisters out. Inheritance is *not* my intent. I don't want *money*. I want family ties − nothing else."

Rod's eyes mellowed. "We are your family, Maggie. Never doubt it."

21

Who Sends a Pocketfull of Posies?

Saturday, July 7th, late morning

THE DOOR TO ROSIE'S POSIES OPENED, setting the little bell into a merry jingle. With a welcoming smile, Rosemary looked at the customer. She put the final touches on a colorful flower arrangement then placed the basket in the center of a circle of clear plastic wrap.

"Is that mine?" the customer asked.

"Yes. You sure got here fast. Is this like what you wanted?"

The customer took a small bag of snack-sized candy bars out of a grocery sack. "Add these, too. Scatter them around."

Rosie cut the bag open and shuffled the little candies throughout the base of the flowers. "How's that?"

The customer nodded. Rosie began picking up the plastic wrap to gather at the top of the basket.

"Where's the happy-face balloon?"

Rosemary thumbed through the order pad. "You didn't order one when you called."

"So? I want one anyway. Add it to the bill."

"Um, I'll go get one right now. Be right back."

Rosemary returned with a bouncy holographic balloon. "This one okay?"

145

"That'll do. Use this for the gift card."

Rosemary took the envelope, slipped it into the forked holder and stuck it in the basket at a jaunty angle. She gathered up the plastic wrap, tied it with a big shiny red bow, and attached the balloon. "How's that?"

"Perfect."

"Will that be all?" Rosemary asked as she handed back the change. "It'll be delivered a little later this afternoon. Is that okay?"

"Perfect."

22

Jobina's Anniversary!

Saturday, July 7th, afternoon

KENT DAVIDSBY ACCEPTED the colorful bouquet basket from the freckle-faced delivery boy. A shaft of afternoon sunlight reflected off the young man's mirror-lens sunglasses.

Jobina peered around the kitchen door. *That boy's a spy! With those x-ray glasses he can see through anything. Be careful, Dad!*

A glittery balloon awash with brilliant colors and an open-mouthed cartoon happy-face bounced in the breeze from the closing door.

"Jobina, it's for you."

"Who sent it, Dad? It isn't my birthday yet … is it?"

"No, it's tomorrow. I don't know who sent it. The card's buried inside." He handed her the heavy basket. "Got it?"

"Uh-huh."

Jobina scuttled along the hall to her room. "That big face, ohmigosh, it's a camera!"

She leaned against the closed bedroom door. Now that she was safe, she examined the basket, turning it around and around.

"Ohmigosh, those shiny colors and bright flowers! Oh,

147

no! They've found me again! No, no, no – it's okay. It's only a disguise! That's it. It's okay, really."

She exhaled a huge breath and plunked down on her bed with the basket in her lap. Covetousness and curiosity overtook caution. She untied the bow and released the balloon. It floated up to the ceiling with its ribbons dancing along on the air current from the ceiling fan. The plastic wrap fell away, and she slid it off the bed onto the floor. Exploring, picking around the flowers, she looked for anything that would give her away to *Them*.

"Can't be too careful, just the same," she mumbled.

Dislodged by the tilting and ransacking of the basket, several of the candies tumbled out.

"What's this? Ohmigosh! A bug? Bugs? Did they send me lots of little Black Boxes this time? No, no, it's okay. These are brown. Ohmigosh, it's candy!"

Jobina ripped one of the little packages open. "Oh, goodie, almond coconut! It's my favorite!" She bounced on the bed with joy at this unexpected treat and popped the whole candy in her mouth. "Yum!"

Snatching two more, she stuffed them into her mouth.

The basket tipped over when she plopped it down beside her on the sagging mattress. The envelope fell out of its holder onto the faded pink chenille bedspread.

Still chomping, she slipped out the note.

She started to read. She stopped bouncing.

> Surprise, Jobina! I am watching.
> Today's my "death anniversary."
> Remember, Jobina? You were there.

I am waiting.

Soon and forever, James

Confused by this message from beyond the grave, she froze in horror, staring at the familiar writing.

The happy-face balloon bounced around the ceiling, ricocheting off the fan blades − thump, thump, thump.

23

Maggie's Goin' Dancing Tonight

Saturday, July 7ᵗʰ, evening

WITHOUT AN EXTENSIVE WARDROBE here from which to choose, Maggie pondered her closet's offerings. A white silk blouse would be perfect with her ankle-length black broomstick skirt and a narrow black leather western-style belt. She pulled on black boots, the tooled leather glove-soft, the silver toe-tips gleaming in the soft light.

She coaxed her hair up with the help of a banana-style comb. Her silver-streaked black waves now just brushed her collar. A bobby pin fell out, and Siam pounced on it.

"Someone must be thinking of me," she said to the cat. Makeup on, then a dot of perfume: "Dune" by Christian Dior, her favorite scent.

With a final tug at her unruly bangs, she added black beaded earrings then slid a sterling silver ear cuff onto her left ear. As she picked up a compact crazy-quilted purse, she heard the soft rumble of CJ's truck coming around the driveway.

Rod, Larkin, and CJ were waiting for her in the Lake Room.

"You look lovely, my dear," Rod said. "Have a wonderful time tonight. You have your key? Cell phone?

Listen to me, I sound like a doting father sending his only daughter on her first date."

"That's all right, Daddy Dear, I kinda like it," she teased, bestowing a kiss on his wrinkled cheek.

"You look mighty fine," CJ said, his smile reflecting his appreciation.

"You clean up very well yourself, cowboy."

He wore knife-edge pressed black jeans, a Western-cut white shirt, black Justins, a dove-gray Stetson, and a big-as-Texas sideways grin.

Oh, that dimple — stop it, silly girl! There's more to look for in a man than a dimple. Look for? Who's looking? She asked herself. *Well, now that you mention it …*

"Are we ready? Then, let's do it. Goodnight, Rod, Larkin."

Rod looked at his wife of over fifty years standing beside him and took her hand in his.

"Good night," they replied in unison.

24

Maggie's Two-Steppin' Blues

Saturday, July 7ᵗʰ, late evening

CINDERELLA'S SLIPPERS WERE TIRED. Never mind Cindy's shoes, Maggie's boots were smokin'. She and CJ had danced to almost every song, sitting out the line dances and free-style. By mutual agreement, they quit the Rusty Anchor right before the last set started. The band was excellent, but the bar had grown louder and smokier, and the dance floor became much too crowded. The typical fare for a spirited Saturday night crowd.

It was half-past Cinderella time. The magic coach was about to turn into a pumpkin. Prince Charming also looked like he might become one, too. Now at Eagles' Rest, they walked under a canopy of stars as they climbed the outer stairs leading to the upper balcony deck.

Feminism be hanged, Maggie loved and appreciated chivalry. Ever the Southern gentleman, CJ unlocked the door to the guest suite and returned her key. She noticed a small patch of dirt close to the door and wondered how it had gotten there.

Distracted by the soft glow of the quarter moon stepping out from behind a cloud, the gentle breezes caressing the trees, and the nearness of the man in the Stetson hat standing beside her, she felt the pull of budding romance. As she turned toward CJ, she stepped in the dirt.

Then everything went boots to breakfast.

The ensuing explosion scared the tar and thunder out of Maggie. She jumped backward and CJ hauled her up close against him.

"What in the world?" she sputtered.

His arm was so tight against her ribcage she had trouble breathing. He released her and pushed her back behind him.

"Get me a flashlight," he ordered.

There was one hanging on a hook by the door. Maggie handed it to him and retreated to the glider swing.

He bent down on one knee, shining the light across the fine grains. "A nasty practical joke, Maggie. It looks like snap powder. It's harmless, except for scaring the bejabbers out of the one who steps on it."

"We s-should call the sheriff."

"I'll talk to him tomorrow. Nothing he can do about it now. No way to find out who put it here, more'n likely." He stood up and set the flashlight on the table. "Are you okay?"

"If my heart rate ever slows down, I will be." She blew out a shaky breath. "If you're not right tuckered, CJ, considering this rude surprise, I don't want to be alone. Would you sit with me for a while and talk? I'd like to wind down, dampen down the decibels, and bask in this balmy weather."

"I'm tired, but definitely not tired of your company. After a scare like that, I wouldn't want to be alone either. Yes, I'll sit a spell with you, as long as you want."

The combination windows were opened to screens during

the summer. Soft breezes filtered in, making sitting outside comfortable. They sat together on the glider swing. A round glass-topped table and four wrought iron chairs were across from them.

Mornings, Maggie liked to sit there with her third cup of coffee and read her Bible. If she and CJ had come in the front door tonight instead, she would have encountered a very rude surprise in the morning. She shivered.

He put his arm around her and pulled her close to him. With her head on his shoulder, listening to the mellow concert of night sounds, Maggie tried to put her racing thoughts back in neutral. *This is nice. But, in a few more days the fairy tale will end. Real pumpkin time.*

"I enjoyed dancing with you tonight, CJ. Thank you for the diversion." Realizing that her statement could be considered an insult, she sat up so fast she bumped his hat and it tilted sideways. "I'm not saying that you are only a nice diversion for this visiting outlander, something you did just to amuse me," she rushed on. "I truly do like your company. But I just realized that in a week I'll be on my way back to Oklahoma."

"Just to Oklahoma? Not home?" He resettled his hat. "Your word choices are telling, Maggie."

"Anymore, I feel that my 'heart home' is here. But my house, my job, and all that entails is there."

He pulled her in closer. She put her head back on his shoulder, where it fit just right.

"Periodically I have business reasons to be in Oklahoma City and Dallas. On my way through, may I call you? Take you out to dinner, or maybe catch a movie?"

"Or have me cook dinner for you?" she questioned with an off-kilter smile.

"Yes, I'd like that. Since I don't have your address or phone number, you'd best give over."

"Only if you'll give over, too," she teased, sitting up. "Come inside."

The sitting room of the guest suite was painted a soft almond and furnished with an elegant feminine décor. At the antique oak secretary, Maggie sat in the cane-seated desk chair. On the desk were her journal and her favorite pen in its protective leather case. From a side drawer she withdrew a small notepad. She removed the pen and began to write.

"My home phone is unlisted, and I give my cell number out to very few people. You are one of the few."

CJ hovered with one hand on the back of her chair, the other flat on the desk, looking over her shoulder.

"You can reach me at the office, ten to five, Monday through Friday. Under no circumstances do I work overtime or weekends."

"There's got to be more to that comment."

"Quite right, there is." She scooted her chair back and CJ straightened up. "I disabused my boss of that notion my very first week there. An hour before quitting time Friday afternoon, Mrs. Allgood announced that a big P.R. campaign project was due on Monday morning. I asked her how long it had been stagnating on her desk. Three weeks, she admitted finally. I said I'd see her on Monday and went home."

"You weren't fired?"

"Thought I would be and don't know why I wasn't," she shrugged. "Except that it was unreasonable, unconscionable, and ludicrous under the circumstances. I've not worked a lick of OT yet, and they've never asked me to."

"You're somethin' else, Maggie." He ran his hand down across his mouth.

"Most of the time, I'm home," she said. She turned in the chair and gave him the paper.

From his jacket pocket he removed a hand-tooled leather card case and slid out a business card. He reached for her pen. It was an old-style Parker pen, solid sterling silver, with a tiny grid pattern etched over the entire barrel, and a gold arrow-shaped clip.

"Where'd you get this pen?" He handed it back to her along with his card.

CJ's question sounded odd, like he was out of breath. Maggie scanned his inscrutable face before answering.

"It was a graduation gift from my high school sweetheart. He hoped it would bring me success in writing."

"Has it?"

"It has brought me many years of pleasurable writing. Success? Maybe. However, I will use it to autograph copies of my 'Best Mystery Novel Ever.' Whenever *that* happens!" She replaced the pen in its case and stood up.

His kiss was as light as moonlight on rose petals.

"That's enough for tonight, child …" Why are these songs running through my head? Not now! I'm busy!

His big hand caressed her cheek. "I could go on for much longer, *mi corazón*, but I'd better go."

Though her knowledge of Spanish was limited, she understood this. Why had he suddenly called her "my heart"?

Standing in the doorway, leaning one shoulder against the doorjamb, she asked him, "Will I see you at church in the morning, uh, later?"

"If it's second service. Now lock up tight. I will talk to Walker tomorrow. Goodnight, Maggie." He spoke her name like a caress, then turned and kissed her again, this time with solid intent.

As he started down the stairs she heard him whistling, *"There's a moon out tonight ..."*

25

Maggie at the Church Picnic

Sunday, July 8th, mid-day

MAGGIE SAT BY HERSELF in the padded pew. The Graceline Bible Baptist Church worship team was singing their special closing song. Both her uncle and aunt sang with the team. Larkin occasionally filled in for the pianist, Joy Blessington, whenever other duties called her away.

Pastor Jeff Blessington, Joy's husband, returned to the pulpit and addressed the fidgety congregation. "The good Lord has blessed us with a mighty fine day today. There's a bit of cloud cover, but no rain is in the forecast to dampen our festivities. I'll say the blessing now because I know that the minute you line up for that bounteous feast outside, getting you folks to stand still then will be like herding cats."

Several good-hearted chuckles followed his comment.

The blessing and God-speed prayers were said, the congregation dismissed, and people disappeared out the front door to the back lawn of the church grounds.

Maggie waited for her relatives to put their music away. "That song was so pretty. I miss singing with a worship team. The small church I attend projects the words on a screen and our pastor leads the singing. When I get in my truck, though, I pop a gospel CD in the player and sing along all the way home."

"That's not the same as being on a team." Rod opened the back door for his ladies.

"No it's not. He preaches expository-style like your pastor does. Instead of a sermon, it's really a Bible study, which I really like. Then he gives an application for today's world."

Four eight-foot tables were all but groaning under the weight of the food. Church folks generally were good cooks, each one known for his or her specialty.

They queued up in line. Rod handed a cafeteria tray to Larkin and Maggie before picking up his own tray.

Maggie found Pattysue and Kaleen in line ahead of her. She handed her tray to Larkin.

"Here, let me help you," Maggie said, taking Pattysue's tray. "It's not easy, juggling with one hand."

"Thank you, Maggie. I'll be some old glad when this cast's off. Then I can get back to doing for myself."

"I fully understand, believe me." Many years ago she'd had a hairline fracture in her left elbow, thanks to a tumble while roller-skating on a concrete floor. Until her arm healed, zipping jeans or dealing with pantyhose were impossible wardrobe issues. Long skirts and sandals were her mainstay that summer. She was thankful it wasn't winter when it happened.

Pattysue patted Maggie's arm. "Thank you. Grandma used to say that denying someone's help would keep a blessing away from the helper."

She looked down at her daughter. Kaleen was standing on tiptoes, eyeing the food. "What do you want to eat,

Kaliebug?"

"Mag-roni salad and a hot dog," Kaleen answered, cradling her teddy bear. "And a choc-lit brownie, please."

Maggie held the tray steady while Pattysue spooned the pasta salad onto her daughter's plate. She then filled her own plate with pasta salad and carrot-raisin salad.

"How about some of Nana Pat's fried chicken instead of a hot dog?" Pattysue asked.

"Yum! Okay, and some carrot stuff like yours." Kaleen was bouncing on the balls of her feet. Her red-gold curls, caught up in pigtails tied with pink bows, jiggled in time.

"Did your sister not come with you today?" Maggie asked.

"She and Coop dropped us off. They went over to visit his parents in Camden today. They'll be back around three or so."

"I hope you are doing all right, Pattysue," Larkin said.

"Uh-huh, we're okay," she answered, spacing her words. "Carrie and Coop are helping. A lot."

The man in line ahead of Pattysue turned and did a double take. "Pattysue Morgan, right?"

At her nod, he continued, "How are you feeling? Is that arm bothering you much? How are you getting along?"

"Hi, Dr. Grayson. I'm fine, except the cast's a nuisance. We're staying with my sister for a while longer. Um, you knew that my husband died?"

"Yeah, I heard about that. I'm sorry, but …" he trailed off.

"I know, Doc, and it's all right. Kaleen and I will be fine."

Kaleen held her teddy bear up for him to take. "See, Teddy's all better. No bandage."

"Good for Teddy," the young doctor said. With gentle fingers, he checked the bear over. "He looks just fine. You're taking good care of him. How are you, young lady?" he asked, passing the bear back to her.

Kaleen developed a case of sudden shyness and hid behind her mother's skirt. She hugged her bear in a death grip.

"Doc, I—"

"Call me Roy, please, Pattysue," he interrupted. "Phone me when you get back home. I'm serious."

He handed her a card, which Pattysue tucked in her pocket. It would keep company with the one he'd given her at the Baywater County Emergency Clinic.

One of the many teenagers milling around detached himself from his friends. He ran over and took Pattysue's tray from Maggie. "I'll take this, Mrs. Morgan. Where you gonna sit?"

"Since you're here by yourself, Pattysue, find a table for the five of us and we'll sit together, okay?" Maggie retrieved her own tray from Larkin.

"If there's room for one more at your table, may I join you?" Roy Grayson asked.

Pattysue agreed and caught Kaleen's little hand. They led the teenager over to a table in the shade of a big oak tree, with the good doctor following close behind.

Maggie scooped carrot-raisin salad and a juicy piece of fried chicken onto her plate. Then she spied a big bowl of crab salad nestled in a larger bowl of ice. She dished up a good-sized spoonful of that rare treat. At the dessert table, she cut a tiny slice of harvest-apple pie, one of Larkin's brownies, and a large spoonful of green-fluffy-stuff, otherwise known as lime gelatin, cottage cheese, and walnut salad.

Rod and Larkin were right behind her, filling their plates with assorted goodies. Together they went to the table where Pattysue, Kaleen, Roy, and several other people were sitting.

The doctor sat beside Pattysue. In between bites of food, he kept up a lively conversation with her and everyone at their table until his cell phone rang.

"Sorry, Pattysue, need to run. Bad accident. Call me, okay?" He grabbed up his trash, shoved it into a large barrel, and took off at a run for the parking lot.

"Mama?"

"Yes, Kaliebug, whatcha need?"

"Where's daddy?" Kaleen asked. Her little eyebrows scrunched up over expressive blue eyes.

The chatter around the table died out.

Pattysue wiped her mouth on a paper napkin. "Sweetheart, he's gone away."

Kaleen climbed into her mother's lap. "Is he coming back?"

Pattysue smoothed the soft golden-red curls away from her little daughter's worried face and murmured, "No, he won't come back, ever."

"Why not?"

A sparrow hopped close to the table, picked up a breadcrumb, and flew away.

"He's dead, sweetheart."

"What's 'dead' mean?"

Pattysue sat for several minutes, gently rocking Kaleen. "It means he's gone to a place far, far away. A place he can never leave."

"Jail?"

"Not ... exactly."

"Is he with Jesus?"

Maggie wondered how Pattysue would field that question. It was a tough one.

"I think Jesus has talked to him." Pattysue kissed the top of Kaleen's head.

"Will we see daddy when we get to heaven?"

"Um, guess we'll find out when we get there."

"Okay," Kaleen said as she scooted over to pick up a fried chicken wing.

A Frisbee flying low across the table broke the tension.

26

Maggie Hears Rod's Story

Sunday, July 8th, late afternoon

MAGGIE SLUMPED in the big club chair. She was as limp as yesterday's news. They had come home after the picnic, sated but overheated.

The comfy, oversized chair offered the drowsy its soft-cushioned lap. Siam purred contentedly on the arm of the chair, imitating a sphinx. Sheba snuffled as she stretched out on the floor beside the chair. The grandfather clock chimed.

Startled, Maggie sat up, disobliging the cat. She rubbed her nose, adjusted her glasses, yawned, and stretched. The book she had been reading slid to the floor, startling the dog.

"Have a nice snooze?" Her uncle was sitting in the companion chair, working another crossword puzzle. Sheba padded over and put her front paws on his knee. He ruffled her soft ears.

"How long was I out?"

He looked at his watch. "About five minutes."

She shrugged. "I don't nap. Now I'm fuzzy-headed." She removed her glasses and wiped them with the hem of her cotton skirt. "I need water. How 'bout you?"

"No, I'm all set, thanks."

She went to the kitchen and returned a few minutes later.

After taking a big drink from a tall glass of water, she sat down. She picked up her book, found her place, and inserted the dust jacket flap as a marker.

Rod smiled and then placed the puzzle and his pen on the table between their chairs. "Tell me, where do you stand, theologically speaking? Still strong?"

She set her glass on the sandstone coaster on the side table. "Oh, yes. God is my Abba Father. Jesus is my Savior. And the Holy Spirit," she laughed, "is my joy giver, my inspiration."

Concerning what church she attended these days, she replied, "Baptist. It's the one organized religion I disagree with the least. When I want answers, the Bible is my first resource. But I still have a long way to go on God's learning curve."

"Haven't we all, m'dear," Rod agreed with a rueful smile.

"What about you?" she asked, her voice gentle. She shifted sideways in her chair, facing him. "What's your story?"

Siam hopped up on the arm of her chair and settled down, his long tail twitching.

Rod cleared his throat. "My parents were Christians, but I didn't grasp the full meaning of the gospel message until I was overseas.

"The transport plane I was in was shot down over Korea. I had barely crawled out when it went up in flames. I was the only survivor. My right leg and left arm were broken. I was helpless. Thankfully, a family of friendly Koreans found me. They took me in, hid me, and patched me up. By luck, or by

God's provision, the father was a medical doctor. He took good care of me. We still stay in touch, after all these years.

"It was two years before I found a MASH unit. Somewhere along the line I'd lost my dog tags. I had the very deuce of a time to convince them I was an American, much less an officer."

"Didn't your Maine accent help prove you were an American?" Maggie asked, caught up in her uncle's story.

"Eventually." Rod shifted in his chair. "During the time I was in Korea, I saw that the God of the Bible I'd grown up knowing about was real and He had a plan for me. His hand was firmly on my shoulder. No matter what happened, God was, and is, always in total control."

"Where did you meet Larkin?"

Rod's face reflected the happy memory. "Larkin was teaching school for the enlisted men's children. We met at the Officer's Club dance. I asked her to dance, and the rest is history, as they say. We got married stateside, and we've been dancing together ever since."

Maggie moved over to sit on the ottoman in front of her uncle's chair. He leaned forward and grasped her slender hands in his slim weathered ones. "The learning curve points toward eternity. M'dear, there's a beautiful heaven waiting. I'm very glad you'll be there with us."

Larkin had walked in, listening without interrupting. When Rod finished talking, she said, "Maggie, dear, the three of us will always be together. Forever." She laid her hand on Maggie's shoulder and squeezed gently. "Supper will be ready in a few minutes."

Larkin's blue eyes met Rod's shining dark green ones.

Exchanging quick nods with her husband, she returned to the kitchen.

Maggie noticed the interplay. Her stomach growled in protest of having been ignored since the picnic, distracting her. She followed her aunt to the kitchen. "Need some help?"

27

Maggie: Shop, Shop, Click

Monday, July 9th, morning

ROD STUCK A TOOTHPICK in the corner of his mouth and leaned back in his chair. "Well, Larkin, m'love, now that we're breakfast-fed and sassy, what are your plans for the rest of the day? Think we'd better go to L.L.Bean's, Maggie? Not too many days yonder and you'll be leaving us."

"Yes, that would be nice. To go to Bean's, I mean! I need chamois shirts in the worst way. I completely wore out the one I had. Right sacrilegious, it is, to have only *one* Bean chamois shirt. The poor thing was beyond threadbare, but I'd had it about fifteen years. This time I'll buy several."

"How hard are the Oklahoma winters?" Larkin was reviewing her shopping list.

"Mild compared to the upper Midwest. It can be pretty cold. We don't have snow very often, but we do have horrible ice storms occasionally. Nasty stuff. Doesn't play nice. Brings everything to a halt, or in a ditch. I might stock up on a few other cold-weather things, too. Ye-up, I'm ready for a trek thataway."

Maggie glanced out the breakfast room window. It was the kind of day that had all the color washed out of it. Shopping would be a good antidote for a gray, dismal day like this. She was more than ready to spend a full day with her relatives.

Siam jumped in Maggie's lap. He stuck his head out begging for a chin scratch, and she obliged him. "With those gorgeous blue eyes, he looks so intelligent."

"He surely is intelligent. Too much so for his own good sometimes," Larkin allowed. "For an indoor cat he's very incurious about the great outdoors. He slipped out one night, and I found him by the north door the next morning, cowering under a basket. That little adventure must have convinced him to remain an inside cat. Sometimes he'll go as far as the edge of the deck when we're out there, but not one step further."

"Maybe a night critter made faces at him, poor baby," Maggie cooed, snuggling the pale gray bundle in her arms. The M marking in the fur above his blue eyes was the single outward evidence of the tabby part of his genetic makeup. His eyes, voice, and temperament were Siamese all the way.

"Yes, poor baby. I'm such a sucker for blue eyes," Larkin admitted, reaching over to pet the cat's brown-tipped gray ears.

"Then why'd you marry me?" her green-eyed husband asked.

"Because I wanted to."

"Good answer, Larkin, m'love." Checking his watch, he added, "We should be getting this show on the road if we're going. Shopping is an all-day affair in this family."

"Do we need to be home any particular time?" Larkin's raised eyebrows matched the guilelessness of her question. "Do you and CJ have plans for this evening?"

Maggie recognized her aunt's subtle matchmaking gambit and grinned. "Nope. I am yours for the whole day."

"Then let's make reservations for dinner tonight at The Pennyroyal. Will you call them, Rod, please?"

"When are we leaving?" Maggie asked her aunt.

"As soon as I change shoes. Be back in five shakes." Larkin was on her way to the master bedroom when the phone rang.

As Larkin halted, Maggie said, "I'll get it!"

"Richardson residence, Maggie speaking."

Silence. Maggie counted to five and was about to hang up when a low voice said, "Go. Away."

"What? Who? Who is this?"

Click. Dial tone.

"Who was that?" Rod asked, peering over the top of his glasses.

"I … don't know." Maggie's brows furrowed like the tilde mark on the far upper left key on the computer keyboard.

"Talk to me," Rod said, reverting to Colonel Richardson mode.

Distracted, she replied, "All they said was, 'Go away.' It sounded like a warning more than a directive."

"Call the sheriff. Here, let me."

She handed him the phone. "There's not much he can do about a short phone call, threatening or not."

"For the record, because of the implied threat, Maggie, I am going to call Walker. Then I'm calling the phone company. We should have had caller ID long before now. I've just been putting off ordering it."

"I'll finish getting ready."

"We'll be on the road as soon as I'm through with these calls," he said, punching in numbers.

* * * * *

"There's no room to put any more stuff in here, Larkin, m'love. I think you both set Bean's inventory back a bit," Rod said as he closed the back hatch of Larkin's van.

"Everybody aboard? I made reservations at The Pennyroyal for tonight. It's a beautiful place on the ocean side of Baywater County, Maggie. Fresh seafood, the best steaks in the county, and a dessert selection that you wish you had room for," Rod said with enthusiasm.

"But they do have take-out boxes," Larkin elaborated, turning in the seat to talk to Maggie. "It's fine dining, so we'll dress accordingly."

"I don't travel without packing for several social options. Now, an evening gown, tux and tails style, I'd have to shop some more."

Rod groaned. "I'm a willing chauffeur, but enough already!"

Larkin said, "I did my part to bolster the economy. We'll have warm things for winter, too."

"There's summer to get through first." Rod adjusted the A/C vents for front and back then turned the fan on high.

"I remember unpacking several skirts, Maggie. The long black one with the pleated lace inserts would be perfect."

"Then I'm all set. What fun! Um, is this a special occasion, or 'just because'?"

Rod glanced at his wife. Following a short pause, he

answered, "We'll call it 'just because.'"

28

Maggie Plays Whodunit

Monday, July 9th, evening

WHEN MAGGIE AND HER RELATIVES entered the reception
area of The Pennyroyal, the hostess greeted them with
flawless diction. She was not tall, but carried herself as if she
were. Her piled-up hair looked like a giant yellow mum had
been plopped on top of her head. Her manner was as
starched as her blouse. A delicate nameplate pinned above
her generous bust stated in an elegant cursive script: C'Anna.

Maggie's cowpoke friends would recognize this as the
kind of place where you trotted out your company manners,
dusted your boots on the leg of your jeans, stood up tall and
straight, and spoke genteel words in a hushed voice.

Walking in the manner of royalty, C'Anna escorted them
toward the airy dining room.

Private alcoves were designed for quiet, intimate
conversations while dining, without the distractions found in
open, public dining rooms. The walls between each alcove
stopped one foot below the ceiling, for air circulation and to
diminish incipient claustrophobia. At the alcove's open front,
blue linen drapes were pulled back into wrought iron
holdbacks. Diners could close the drapes for added privacy if
they wished to do so. Across from the alcoves, a dramatic

wall of windows assured every diner stunning views of the Atlantic Ocean.

On a folded white card, a calligrapher had written in blue-ink copperplate: Reserved ~ Richardson. The Pennyroyal's hostess removed the sign. Her eyes were the color of burnt coffee, and the look she gave Maggie was the temperature of yesterday's brew, iced.

The round table was dressed with a blue linen tablecloth and matching napkins. Shimmering cut crystal goblets caught the light and returned diamond sparkles. A nearly translucent china cup and saucer and a red rose floating in a crystal bowl were at each place setting.

Low lighting, soft and romantic, was not so dim that one couldn't decode the menu, or more to the point, decipher what was on one's plate.

The c-shaped crinkles around their waiter's mouth were like happy parentheses suggesting a healthy sense of humor. "Welcome to The Pennyroyal. I'm Eric. What beverages may I bring you this evening?"

Eric passed menus to each of them with a hint of a flourish before dashing off with their drink orders.

Maggie stared at the cup and saucer, brows furrowed.

Larkin leaned forward and whispered, "I already did. It's English bone china."

Maggie giggled in surprise. "How'd you know I wanted to peek?"

"We've been in each other's back pockets for over two weeks. I know that look, dear."

Eric brought their drinks and was now poised with pen and miniscule notebook ready to take their orders. To Larkin, he nodded and said, "Ma'am?"

"Baked scallops, please, steamed asparagus, and the twice-baked potato."

He turned to Maggie. "For you, ma'am?"

"Lobster *au naturel*, please," she answered with one eyebrow quirked upward.

Eric asked, straight-faced, "Lobster in the rough?"

Maggie blinked and looked over the top of her glasses at the waiter, catching the mischievous twinkle of a kindred spirit. *Okay!*

"If you mean straight off the trawler still swimming, not quite," she said in a mock snobby manner. "Neither do I have a wish to be formally introduced to my meal beforehand. Steamed, drawn butter but no fancy sauces. Simply put, don't ruin a good thing. Baked potato. Leave the foil, if you use it, in the kitchen, please. Double butter, I mean real butter, not margarine. No sour cream. Steamed asparagus for me, too." She smiled, the corners of her mouth twitching, ready for a fit of laughter. "Thank you, please."

Grinning, Eric jotted down Maggie's order. Composing a straight face, he turned to Rod. "Sir?"

Rod deferred to the restaurant's signature prime-cut steak. "Make it medium rare, with grilled mushrooms and glazed onions. I'll have a baked potato with double butter and sour cream on the side. Thank you."

"It seems you're no stranger to the idiosyncrasies of menus or the nuances of descriptive copy." Larkin's smile lit up her face.

"One of my wilder assignments as a free-lance writer was to critique fashionable, trendy restaurants. 'The Mystery

Diner strikes again!' I learned to read every word on the menu for what it means, not what one hopes it will say, and to ask point-blank questions. Most of the time I ate well, but I carried bicarb tablets, just in case."

Muted conversations with an occasional ripple of laughter drifted through the elegant surroundings. The trio took little notice of the hostess walking by with three couples that she established in the alcove next to theirs.

Eric delivered their dinners, steaming hot and smelling wonderful. After Rod said grace, they forestalled conversation for several minutes to focus their attention on their meals.

Larkin laid down her knife. "At the picnic yesterday, I had a chance to talk to Pattysue alone for a few minutes."

"How's she doing?" Rod asked, cutting a bite of steak.

"She seems to be doing better, both physically and emotionally." Larkin shook pepper on her potato. "Carrie is being harassed by phone calls from their cousin Jobina, she told me. Afterward, Carrie lets off steam by rehashing the conversation with Pattysue. She said that was 'too much drama' for her."

"Pattysue seems like a quiet, gentle person," Maggie said. She had cracked the legs and claws and was ready to dig out the lobster meat. She wiped her hands on the wet hand towel that was provided for diners who chose shellfish for their dinners.

Larkin cut a succulent scallop in half. "She is a sweet young woman. She wants to go home soon. Back to her quiet little cottage."

"Ready to get on with her new life," Rod said. "Good for

her. She's got gumption. Got to watch those quiet ones."

They discussed Morgan's murder between bites of the excellent dinner. In the manner of a Mystery Dinner Theater, they assigned made-up names for the cast of characters and wrestled the whodunit and why. Too much fun, it was, while it could have been slanderous if the wrong people, or dangerous if the right person, had been listening.

Not quite the loftiest dinner topic for the fine dining environs of The Pennyroyal, perhaps. They tamped down their enthusiasm so as to not upset the rarified atmosphere. However, Maggie was sure that Colonel and Mrs. Richardson would never be kicked out of any establishment they graced with their presence.

"There's the Fruitcake," Rod suggested. "Complexes galore. Jobina could be sneaky enough to do the Deed Dirty and intelligent enough to shift the blame to someone else."

"Possibly," Larkin hedged, wiping her lips on the linen napkin. "What about Oily Limp Wrist? You know, Victor Turner and the Mob connections with Deeds Most Foul."

"Hmm, I hadn't thought about Victor being involved. CJ mentioned that he was shooting a wedding over in Scarboro a while back, and he saw Bob and Victor together." Rod retrieved his napkin from the floor. "Their body language was eloquent although he couldn't hear a word they were saying."

Eric brought their postprandial coffee in a silver carafe and poured a cup for each of them. The moment he departed, they returned to their drama.

"What about the pearl I found near where the body had been?" Maggie asked. "I told you about my run-in with

Victor after the funeral? I noticed one of his cufflinks was missing a pearl. At the baby shower, Carrie wasn't wearing her pearl necklace, the twin to Pattysue's."

C'Anna passed by with a young couple lagging behind, holding hands, with adoring looks for only each other.

Seconds later, she was standing in their alcove. "Is everything to your satisfaction this evening? May we bring you anything else? Shall I set aside desserts for you to take home?" she inquired with cold, distant politeness.

Assuring her that everything was fine, as always, Rod ordered three desserts to go.

C'Anna departed, and Larkin picked up the story line. "It appears to be an opportunistic kind of murder. Not preplanned and certainly not professional."

"Premeditated, in the sense of stalking, waiting for opportunity, and acting on impulse when the chance presented itself," Maggie allowed. "Would that be ambushed or bushwhacked?"

"Good question," her uncle answered, setting down his cup. "Bushwhacked, probably, though both words mean the same. If this were the Badlands, either would have been a moot point for the hanged man."

"Excuse me." C'Anna presented the bill on a vintage crystal celery plate that she placed beside Rod's coffee cup. He put his credit card on the plate.

"Thank you. I will be right back." She paused at the doorway, waiting for Eric to pass with a loaded tray balanced on his shoulder.

"What about Cooper, Carrie's husband? He's been behind the scenes this whole time. What shall we call him?"

Larkin asked. "Oh, I know, he's Gallant Knight. He does have that Sir Galahad look about him."

"I would presume Cooper loves his wife," Maggie answered just as C'Anna returned.

Rod picked up his credit card and signed the bill. "Thank you."

"You're welcome. Your desserts are waiting at the front desk," she announced, her voice colder than a hard winter. She turned on her heels and quit the alcove.

"Well! She's copping an attitude and a half tonight," Maggie said with spirit.

"It is very unusual behavior for the Pennyroyal's staff. We've always had excellent service, though we've never been here on a Monday before. She is not our regular weekend hostess," Rod said.

"Where were we?" Maggie asked, eager to return to their dining armchair sleuthing.

"We can hope there are no love triangles there," Larkin said, picking up where they left off. "Fair Maiden is loved, because she's family and is a nice person, and Gallant Knight adores little Kaleen. They don't have any children. I understand that Carrie isn't interested in motherhood."

"What about Gallant Knight, who is angry that Fair Maiden and Small Child have been hurt, so he wants revenge?" Rod suggested.

"Casting Pattysue as Fair Maiden, that fits her persona. What about The Woman Scorned? She was that, but violence is so out of character for her," Larkin said.

"I have a hunch it's a woman." Maggie's cup made a tiny plink on the saucer.

"Why's that?" Rod laid his napkin on the table.

"It's too neat. Like one step removed. A man might contemplate applying major mayhem to the object of his anger."

"More'n likely," Rod agreed. "Though someone of Victor's small stature might prefer doing the deed one step removed, too."

"Quite so. Victor's a possibility. I've never liked or trusted him. Him behind bars is a pleasant thought." Maggie paused and took a different tack. "I like Pattysue and think we could be friends. Can't quite cotton to her sister, though."

She thought about their brief encounter at the baby shower. "It wasn't just her sloppy way of dressing, there was something off-putting about her. Wasn't it Agatha Christie who wrote about 'something evil this way comes'?"

"I believe so," Larkin answered. "'By the pricking of my thumbs,' is how the rhyme begins."

"I often get those classic authors mixed up. I've read all of Agatha Christie's books several times. Never do get tired of them."

"So, mystery authors aside, whodunit? Someone on our list, or the mysterious, all-purpose X?" Larkin queried, steering the conversation back to the main topic.

"I'm leaning toward the Mother/Sister person." Maggie propped an elbow on the table with chin in hand, genteel manners abandoned for undivided attention on an intriguing subject. "Carrie's so protective of Pattysue. Might do anything to keep her safe."

The sun was well past the yardarm. Passing its radiance through the glass wall, it washed the room with fiery essence as it kissed the horizon good night. Rod suggested that it would behoove them to make tracks for home.

"Ready, ladies? It has been very enjoyable, but the day has grown a beard."

Rod held Larkin's chair first, then Maggie's. He tucked a lady's arm under each of his. They walked toward the front desk. Looking first at Larkin then at Maggie, he said with obvious pride, "Here I am with a beautiful woman on each arm. Not too many men my age can brag about that!"

They drove away from The Pennyroyal with three individual containers of Pennyroyal Double Mudslide Cake awaiting their midnight munchies.

During the trip back to Eagles' Rest, Maggie stared out the side window. It was late evening with some moonlight, but not enough light to see very well. Houses with false sunshine leaking out of the windows from around closed curtains, chasing away shadows, watching, watching. The wind sighing, sighing. The trees whispering, whispering.

Waxing poetic with the purple prose again, she thought. *I really am tired.*

29

Maggie Talks of Wishes and Horses

Monday, July 9th, late evening

HOME ONCE MORE, they settled down in the Lake Room. Rod opened a bottle of wine. "Helps to settle the tummies," he said, passing half-full glasses around.

Perpendicular to the fireplace, two loveseats faced each other, with a granite-topped wrought iron coffee table between them. Rod and Larkin sat together. Maggie and the cat sat across from them.

"You ready for your flight Sunday, Maggie?" Rod asked, leaning back on the loveseat beside his wife.

Maggie slipped off her heels, wiggled her toes, and took a hearty sip of the mellow wine.

"Don't want to think about that now. Anyway, it's a late morning flight. You won't need to get up before you even go to bed just to take me to the airport. You're awfully good to do it, though."

"We got you here," Rod answered, "and we'll get you back. Don't worry."

Maggie wondered if "getting her back" was a double entendre, but probably not.

"I'll land in Oklahoma City fairly late. My neighbor will meet me at the airport. I won't go back to work until

Tuesday. I took an extra day to make up for the Fourth," she explained, twisting a lock of hair.

Rod looked askance at her. "Do you really want to go?"

She sat very still for a space of time, thinking about an appropriate answer. A "yes" might suggest she was eager to go home. A negative could put pressure on her to do something she wasn't ready for − or was she?

She opted for the truth. In a small voice, she replied, "No."

Larkin was fingering her half-carat diamond wedding ring in what Maggie recognized as an unconscious gesture. Rod glanced at his wife. She raised one eyebrow in a silent answer.

"Maggie, if you could do whatever you wanted, with money being no object, without any fine print, what would you like to do most of all?"

"If 'wishes were horses,' you mean, Uncle Rod?" Maggie tapped a French-manicured fingernail on her bottom lip.

The grandfather clock near the front door, relentless and reliable, ticked away the minutes.

Maggie tucked her long legs underneath her. The cat jumped up on the back edge of the loveseat. Siam settled down, purring a love song in her ear.

"Without a doubt, I would move here to Baysinger Cove, or a town real close by. Might have my own business. Or write the World's Best Mystery Novel." She twirled her hair and wondered if any of her dreams would ever be realized.

"What kind of business?"

The eagerness in her aunt's voice snapped Maggie back

to the present. She swung her long legs down and scooted to the edge of the couch. "I think maybe, an embellishment kind of store? With beads and buttons, laces and ribbons, and assorted doodads? Oh, you know what I mean. A purveyor of ephemera and stuff and lots of it."

Larkin's smile was benevolent. "I do believe so, Maggie."

Warming to her theme, Maggie's whole being was awake with enthusiasm. "Yes, fun stuff for beaders, crazy quilters, maybe even art doll makers, mostly embellishers in general. Since I am proficient in those areas, too, who would be better than *moi*," she said, pointing toward herself, "to cater to that type of clientele?"

"I would be your best customer. Seriously, Maggie dear, I do believe there's a strong enough customer base here in the area that you would do well. Long, dreary, snowy winter days are not spent idle, you know. We need this kind of a store, like we discussed the other day."

Larkin continued, her own enthusiasm showing all over her face, "Furthermore, I could help you with the shop. You know I owned an antique store for many years, which gave me first-hand experience with the nuances of retail. Rod has a good head for math. He could handle the cash register and do odd jobs and what-not."

"What my darling wife means is, I'm pretty handy with a hammer and doing mechanical and technological things." Rod rose and walked over to the stereo wall. He chose a CD and slipped it in the player. "And if I can't do it, I know a lot of talented local people who can."

Just above a whisper, Acker Bilk's soulful clarinet

drifted through the room.

"Whoa, whoa, slow down, folks! It's a grand idea. But right now I can't afford to quit my day job, as they say, and make such a drastic move." Maggie slumped back in her seat. "Oh, razzlefratz!" She blew an upward breath that ruffled her bangs. "But do I ever wish."

Rod returned and stood beside her. "Ayuh, it may only be a dream right now, Maggie, m'dear, but don't you ever let go of it. Without a dream, you don't have a vision. Without a vision there is no goal. Without a goal, you won't know where you're going or that you've arrived." Rod grasped Maggie's hands and pulled her up. He brushed a kiss across her forehead.

"Don't ever give that dream up, Maggie. Remember, we're here for you whenever you need us. Family."

"I know, Uncle Rod. You two are the only family I have, and that *is* what matters."

"I loved your grandparents, my parents, very much. We miss them, but they are in Heaven, waiting for us." Rod moved to sit down beside his wife. "There are not many of us left, m'dear."

Maggie eased herself down onto the loveseat, nudging the cat out of the way, and picked up her wine glass. "I miss Grandmother and Grandfather, too. They were right brave to take on the raising of me, a toddler, in their sunset years."

For a space of time, only the clarinet's mellow melodies floated in the air.

Rod sat forward, his hands clasped as if in prayer. "We were overseas when you went to live with them. In one of Mother's letters, she told us how Marion dumped you on

185

their doorstep in Deer Hill, with your little brown suitcase in hand. You were four when they took full custody of you and moved to North Belgrade. We would have interceded, but you were settled in and we didn't want to disrupt your life."

"Even so, you were always there for me, weren't you?" Maggie asked, tears filling her eyes. Tears: condensation created when a warm heart meets a cold world. Some of the missing pieces of her puzzling young years fell into place.

"We tried to be," he said. "We are now."

She watched her uncle walk to the bay window. In the pale moonlight, Old Man Mountain was simply a bulky shadow in the distance.

A few minutes later he turned around and said, "Rita called the other day about a cottage on Cranberry Lane that's just come on the market."

"Yes, Aunt Larkin mentioned it."

"Out of curiosity, we went to look it over. The owners are very anxious to sell. It's on two acres, with frontage on Serenadelle Lake. The land itself is worth more than the seventy-five thousand they're asking for it. The structure is sound, but it could use some modernizing."

"A serious scrubbing alone would work wonders," Larkin added, wrinkling her nose. She related tales of the dust and cobwebs running amok in an unoccupied house.

Maggie opened her mouth to speak, but Rod put up a cautionary hand. "We are cognizant of your fiercely independent spirit," he said. "There is also a detached two-car garage with an efficiency apartment above it."

"Where are you going with this?" Maggie asked. She put her wine glass on the coffee table.

"You mentioned starting a business here. That house would be just perfect for it, and it's in a great location," Larkin explained. "It's near the old train depot. That's a very busy place with the Art at the Depot there now."

"It's very tempting," Maggie admitted, taking a hankie out of her pocket, realizing their kind intentions coupled with her indecision could add up to stormy personal weather. Torn between one thing and another, her tears were too near the surface not to have a backup plan. She understood that her folks were just being supportive. She should be gracious and acknowledge their concern. But, still …

"Thank you for checking out the house. I appreciate that you're trying to help me. That's way more money than I could liquidize, if that's even a word. Part of that is in my bungalow. If I could even sell it in this down market."

"Could you rent it?" Larkin drained her wine glass and shook her head at Rod's question for more.

Maggie shuddered. "I hate the thought of being a landlord. It's worse being this far removed."

"Not practical," Larkin agreed, setting her empty glass on the coffee table.

Maggie was suspicious of her aunt's sudden acquiescence. "I've got some money in various CDs and money market accounts, but that's my safety cushion, not to be spent. I must work for at least another ten years, just so I won't get bored or have to schlep around in a cardboard box when I do retire. Benefits? Got to have those. I *am* getting older." She twisted a strand of hair around her fingers. "Although I may not have a job when I get back to Oklahoma."

Larkin leaned forward. "What do you mean?"

"I told you about the troubles I'm having with my job. Last Friday, I received an email from my boss. Seems that Elbert-Brat crashed the computer, and she was in a tizzy. Mrs. Allgood ordered me to catch the next flight out."

"You're still here, obviously," Rod said, returning from his window-gazing.

"I will not give in to a bully. If there is a confrontation after I get back to the office, I will be even more rebellious. I did disobey her directive, though not directly. I ignored it. She had no right to even ask. Gave her two solutions to the immediate problem and said I'd see her on the seventeenth."

"She hasn't answered you?" Larkin asked.

"I've not heard anything from her since." Maggie let go of her hair. "Maybe God's trying to get my attention."

"Perhaps, dear, He is. It would be easy to start up a business here, like we've been discussing," Larkin said. "You know we want you to be here, near us." She hesitated. "Or would CJ be the one to tilt the scale our way?"

Maggie recognized the hopeful ace card Larkin was playing. "CJ has already tilted my scale, and my windmill." She saw her aunt's eyes open wider and interpreted the hopeful glint. "No wedding bells, Aunt Larkin, please! I like him a lot, and he's easy company. I'm just not ready for a man to be the main focus of my life right now, not in that way."

"Child, it is entirely possible to have a close relationship with a man and have no romantic overtones," she scolded in her sternest Southern-lady manner.

"He's got me bumfuzzled."

"How so?" Larkin asked.

"He reminds me so very much of someone I knew long ago. Maybe a classmate, but I can't place him. The name isn't right, so he's not who I thought he might be. Which is all right since I like him for himself, regardless. No more tilting at windmills for me. The steady course beckons." Maggie stood and stretched like a cat.

Siam jumped down, stretched in languid cat fashion, mirroring Maggie, then sashayed toward the kitchen.

"We love you, Maggie. Don't fret. The answers will come. Go, get some sleep, and we'll spend your remaining days here doing whatever you want." Larkin's voice caught. "Let's not be away from each other so long in the future."

Hugging first her aunt, then her uncle, Maggie whispered good night. With one foot on the stairs, she turned and said, "I love you both, more than you know. I thank God for you. And thank you for loving me back."

30

Maggie Finds S-S-Sweets, My Sweet?

Tuesday, July 10ᵗʰ, morning

THE NEXT MORNING, MAGGIE came downstairs and walked toward the kitchen carrying a package, her eyebrows quirked in a perplexed frown.

"What have you got there, dear?"

"A candy box, Aunt Larkin. But it looks funny. Odd funny."

"Why, there's no outer plastic wrapper on it. Only the ribbon is holding it together," Larkin exclaimed. "I know recycling has become the Right Thing to Do, but for candy boxes?"

"Where'd you find it?" Rod was on his way from the breakfast room to join them in the kitchen.

"On the deck. I went out there to thank the Lord for another day. A chair was placed directly in front of the door. No way I could have missed it. This was on the seat."

"Did you hear anyone outside last night?" Rod asked. "You didn't happen to look out before you went to bed, did you?"

"Nope. Washed up, climbed into bed, and read for a bit."

"That looks sort of like CJ's writing," Rod peered at the box without touching it. "I'll call him," he said, reaching for the phone.

"Hello, CJ. Rod here. Maggie found an anonymous package outside her door this morning. Did you leave something there?" ... "Didn't think so. I'll ..."

Maggie yelped, jumped, and threw the box on the floor. "It m-moved!" She stopped backing up when she bumped up against the refrigerator door.

Five minutes later Sheriff Bainbridge arrived, lights flashing, with CJ's truck almost on the cruiser's back bumper.

Curious to a fault, Maggie went outside with the men, albeit at a very cautious distance. The general consensus agreed it wasn't a bomb, as was deduced from its wiggle factor.

The sheriff placed the box on a rock down by the shore. His actions afforded the package the benefit of the doubt. With a pocketknife, he sliced the ribbon. He stepped back at the same moment the lid popped off. A very unhappy, very skinny, very green garden snake slithered out of the box, zigzagging its way Speedy-Gonzales-style to the nearest crevice and disappeared.

Maggie, at first glimpse of the snake, had beat-feet straight to the safety of the lower front deck. Her face was as white as her blouse. She sat with her legs bent and her arms wrapped around her knees.

"Relatively harmless." CJ strode across the lawn toward Maggie.

"N-not when you're t-terrified of them, it isn't!"

CJ sat down beside her and put his arm around her shaking shoulders.

"No, it isn't," the sheriff said. "Some call it harassment. One look at your face, and I call it personal terrorism. Period. We'd better go inside. Let's talk." He reached out, taking her hand to help her up.

To Maggie's mind, two of the scariest words spoken to either a child or adult were: "Let's talk."

Maggie was scared, and admitted it.

"These things," she said, referring to terrorizing campaigns, which during the last sixty minutes she had learned more about than she ever wanted to know, "why are they happening to me in the first place? I don't get it."

"First things first, Maggie. Who knows about your snake phobia?"

"Only my entire family and every second kid I went through school with, Walker." It was exasperating, considering the wide range of possible deed doers.

Larkin set a cobalt blue mug in front of Maggie. With a loving smile, she nodded her thanks to her aunt.

"Any specific incidents come to mind?" the sheriff asked. He had a pen and a notepad out on the table, already covered with his distinctive script.

Maggie wrapped her hands around the mug and took a cautious sip of aromatic hazelnut coffee. After a long pause, she said, "Once, a small grass snake slithered across the kitchen floor. I totally freaked. Marion laughed at me. My sister, Beryl, made fun of me and egged the other two sisters on to razz me, too. After that, Beryl would hunt for anything she could use to taunt me." Maggie hesitated, caught up in the memory. "I kept quiet about anything else that was frightening to me. Wasn't about to provide her with any extra ammunition."

"Why was she so mean in the first place?" Larkin asked. "That's wicked."

"Bless me, I wish I knew." Maggie shrugged. "Beryl hated me as much as her mother did. Marion's dead and none of her daughters are around here, as far as I know, or care. I can't figure why Beryl would be doing this now, if she were the one doing it. Could be, I suppose, Morgan's murderer may be trying to scare me off."

She took another sip of coffee before the realization of what she had said hit her. "Yikes!"

"It's a small town, Maggie. You know how things are overheard and passed on," CJ said, peering into his cup with the intensity of a tealeaf reader seeking inspiration or insects.

"Yes, I'm seeing personally the bad side of just what you mean." Her voice was low, anger echoing her words.

"That first anonymous phone call, did you recognize the voice?" Walker laid his big hand on her slender one and patted it.

"Not the voice. But I'll bet it was Cousin Victor's big dude buddy who called." She told him how she'd taken a guess, challenged the caller, and hit pay dirt.

"What about the second one, Monday morning?"

"I can't place it. It was a woman, though."

"How can you tell?"

"The pitch and timbre, Sheriff. A woman's voice differs from a man's. I'm musically oriented, so my ear is more finely tuned, I guess." Unable to sit still any longer, she slid out of her chair and started pacing back and forth across the opening between the breakfast room and kitchen.

"Other than all over the devil's half-acre, where have you been since Morgan's murder, where you could have been overheard?" the sheriff asked. He scooted his chair around to watch her and crossed his long legs at the ankles.

"Dining and dancing with CJ. Dinner at The Pennyroyal with my folks. At the DQ, or at the Sawmill Hill Cafe, just about everywhere. Oh, Walker, I don't know!" she fussed. "This is right scarifying."

She raked her fingers through her mussed-up hair and headed to the kitchen for another cup of coffee. How many cups was that now? Six? Seven? *Yeowser, I'd better switch to water before I start java jump jiving.*

Empty-handed, she rejoined her family and friends. "I speak my mind. I'm not PC and will go to my grave *not* being politically correct. The term itself is an oxymoron." Taking a deep breath, she elaborated, "I *am* inclined to get up on soapboxes, like I am now." She pulled at a lock of hair then returned to the kitchen for the forgotten glass of water.

CJ said, "We were at the Rusty Anchor last Saturday night. We discussed the murder during the band break. It was so noisy in there it would've been hard for anyone to overhear us. One couple behind us was sitting so close that when the woman stood up, she banged Maggie's chair hard. A busy night, the tables were packed close in. They might have heard snatches, I reckon."

"Did you know them?" Walker unwound his legs. Picking up the coffee carafe, he poured another cup of coffee. He helped himself to a doughnut from the Stellar Bakery box.

"No, can't say as I did. Don't think they were

townsfolk," CJ said, dusting doughnut crumbs from his napkin onto his plate.

"We three went to The Pennyroyal for dinner last night. Among other things, we discussed the murder in the manner of a Mystery Dinner Theater and whom we might tag for the star role." Rod smiled. "We got kind of silly about it and laughed a lot."

Walker swallowed and asked, "Who got the starring role?"

Rod polished his glasses on the hem of his three-button pullover shirt. He checked for spots on the lenses before slipping them back on. "I was tagging the nutty Jobina Court, but Maggie was plumping for Carrie, citing mother instinct. Cooper, we dismissed him out of hand. At one point Larkin was opting for the oily Victor Turner, but later she sided with Maggie's view." He laughed, recalling the fun they'd had together, dining out as a family. "And in the end, I had to agree with Maggie. Her reasoning has merit."

The rumbling of a heavy vehicle slowing to make the turn in the circular driveway and a light thump caught Rod's attention. "That's Jimmy, delivering my paper. He's late today. That man needs to get his muffler fixed."

He started to rise but Maggie stopped him. "I'm already up. I'll get your paper."

Just shy of the doormat was the newspaper, and …

Three red roses.

Roses tied with a shiny black ribbon.

Dead roses.

"Oh, no!" she cried, clamping her hands over her mouth. Just as she began to back up, CJ reached her. She turned and burst into hysterical tears.

CJ scooped her up and carried her into the Lake Room. They sat down in the big club chair. He held her, hunkered down beside him, until she quieted.

"Hush, *mi corazón*, I'm here," CJ whispered in her hair.

"Oh, CJ, I don't usually indulge in hysterics," she said, her voice thick with emotion.

I tossed Cousin Victor on his education at the Shindig. Dead flowers on the doorstep, and I'm a shivering mass of feminine indignation? Gathered into the family fold should not have upset anyone. Should it? Maybe I am due for a nice, quiet, nervous breakdown.

"A nervous breakdown is neither in my genetic makeup nor part of my agenda for the immediate future," she said in between sighs and snuffles.

"I just don't get it! What is the purpose of this insidious, intangible, campaign? I can't *fight* what I can't *see*!" With her mini-tantrum exhausted, her emotional equilibrium was reasserting itself. She dragged a hankie out of her pocket and blew her nose.

"What about my innate sense of curiosity? Has that upset someone? I've already figured out whodunit! I think. Or maybe I have fingered the wrong person and—"

"Maybe so, Maggie. Walker and his crew are on the murderer's trail," CJ said, interrupting her jeremiad.

"These incidents may be tame harassment by definition, but very frightening to someone who has had little contact with the evil side of inhumanity. *No* contact would make me exceedingly happy right now," she said, winding down.

Other thoughts kept the mad merry-go-round in her head

196

revolving, constant, and redundant. Maggie often wondered if the circus calliope was what insanity sounded like. *At least, there is no maniacal calliope playing in the background. Therefore, I am still sane.*

She was terrified, furious, and downright frustrated. Snuggled here with CJ, warm, solicitous, and protective, was comforting. That thought was bit unsettling, but something sane and tangible she could deal with later. *Mañana – just not today.*

CJ put his hand in the small of her back as she attempted to extract herself from the cushy club chair. With that helpful nudge she managed to gain her feet. She went upstairs to her room and washed her face. The mirror reflected a mature face marred with tears and a red nose. No makeup could repair this chaos. *Oh well.*

She tossed her sodden hankie in the laundry basket and took a fresh one from the antique glove box on the dresser. Feeling totally drained and fragile, she trudged downstairs and followed CJ, who was on his way to the breakfast room.

Rod was a retired Air Force Colonel, Military Intelligence, and CID. Even now, his military manner, as quick as a smart salute, snapped to attention.

"Jimmy Howe left your paper. Is there any reason for him to have delivered the roses, too?" Walker asked.

"None. Morgan had an affair with Jimmy's wife. If anything, Jimmy would pin a medal on the person who killed Morgan, not harass my niece."

"When you were at The Pennyroyal, did you recognize any of the other diners?"

"Here in Baywater County, that answer could be

'everyone,' as you well know," Rod said. "People from out of the area don't typically dine there during the week, especially on a Monday. There were three couples dining in the alcove right next to ours. They had pulled their curtain for privacy, therefore we couldn't see them anyway."

"Anything else?"

"As a matter of fact, an odd thing happened there, now that I think about it. The hostess was a haughty number." Rod described the woman much as Maggie had captured it in her own mind's eye. "Odd name, too: C'Anna. She was polite to a fault. I saw the stone cold look she gave Maggie. Uncalled for, I thought. We usually go there on a weekend, though, so she wasn't our regular hostess."

"Her makeup was heavy and looked like it was done by a professional artist. An about-face change of clothing and a drastic difference in hairstyle can be an effective disguise. Makeup doesn't change bone structure, though." Maggie said. "She reminds me of someone I saw recently, but I can't remember where."

31

Maggie, Whatcha Think?

Wednesday, July 11th, morning

"**HI, GUYS, COME ON IN.** Want some coffee? It's fresh," Maggie coaxed.

"Ayuh, thank you. Get us some of that good brew and let's sit for a bit outside. The morning's too nice to ignore," Sheriff Walker Bainbridge answered.

CJ Dubois took her hand in his.

"Hello, CJ. It's nice to see you again." *Dang, he's handsome. Oh, I can't be blushing again – at my age, yet!*

"Nice to see you, too, Maggie," he said with a Texas-wide grin. "Maine air sure puts roses in your cheeks."

After retrieving her hand, Maggie went to the cupboard for two stout pottery mugs. She poured coffee, handed a mug to each of the men, and refreshed her own. They walked to the sun porch, which was an all-season affair that enclosed the southern end of the house.

The lawman sat on the padded, solid oak, old church pew. CJ eased his long frame into an Adirondack chair. Maggie settled in the glider swing facing the men.

Siam jumped into CJ's lap, almost upsetting his coffee. CJ set the mug on the wide arm of the chair, settled the cat down with an efficient turnabout move, and began to scratch the furry chin.

"How are people acting around you?" The sheriff referred to her snooping at the crime scene, that newsy tidbit being all over town.

"I've been made nice to by the people I've met. Most of them anyway." *Other than villainous Victor and his unfounded accusations, she couldn't imagine who else ...*

"Maggie? Where are you?" asked the sheriff.

"Oh, sorry. Woolgathering. Say again?"

"What do you mean by 'most of them'?" Walker asked.

Maggie reminded them of the incidents with Victor and the harassing phone calls. "I wonder if he's responsible for the impractical jokes, too?"

"Most of the fingerprints were smudged. As for the ones we could lift, there are no records. The snap powder itself is impossible to trace."

"Hmmm."

"Anything else you've picked up around town? Besides new friends?"

"And maybe a few enemies, Walker?" Maggie added. "Well, I've been gone for so long, everything here is relatively new. Mostly I'm clueless whom they're talking about, so I'm not much help to you there."

"What do you know about the Morgans?"

She pushed one foot on the floor, setting the glider swing into motion, tugged at a strand of hair, and considered his question. Sheba padded over and plopped down under the swing, her tail thumping the floor.

"The Sunday afternoon I arrived here, we were at the Sawmill for a late lunch. That was the first time I ever laid eyes on them. Pattysue and Kaleen were bandaged up. Larkin introduced us. We learned that Pattysue's husband had been the deed-doer. Kaleen had wanted some of their cookies, which is why Pattysue and Kaleen were at the cafe."

"'If I were married to him, I'd be a widow,'" the sheriff quoted. He leaned forward on the bench, watching her like a cat does a mouse.

Maggie stopped in mid-swing and let go of her hair.

CJ stopped petting the cat.

She took a deep breath and returned his stare. "It is no secret that I have absolutely no use for men who are abusers. There are places for these victims to go, safe houses. There must be shelters, even here in this neck of the woods, if the victims can overcome fear and walk away. I know it's not always that simple. Me, I would leave. Somehow." She crossed her arms with her hands on opposite shoulders, hugging herself. She slid her hands down to cup her elbows and leaned forward.

"My life is too precious to me, and I would find a way out." She dropped her arms and gripped the seat of the swing. "I hope never to be so desperate as to want, or need, to take another person's life. No man is worth spending my life in prison for. No, I did not kill him, Sheriff. I have never even met the man. Whoever did it had no legal right to take his life." She looked out the window at the mountain beyond the lake and felt peace descending in her spirit.

"Why not 'no moral right'?" the lawman asked.

Good catch, she thought, *to single out that small distinction.* Looking straight at him, she slowed her words down. "Because I'm not sure it wasn't."

The antique wall clock chimed the hour.

CJ resumed petting the cat.

The big lawman settled back on the bench and drank his coffee.

Maggie started up the swing again.

"I have to consider everything, Maggie. Here you arrive on a Sunday, make a compromising comment, and three days later Pattysue Morgan is a widow. It's a process of elimination, clearing suspects and narrowing the field."

"I understand."

"As a rule, I don't approve of amateur sleuths muddying the water of an investigation. However, something can be gained by listening to the viewpoint of someone outside the boat," the sheriff said. "Whom do you suspect and why?"

Maggie was impressed that he did not mix his metaphors. She sipped her cooling coffee while she organized her thoughts. "Pattysue couldn't have done it, if the truck was the method. Not with a broken arm."

"Except that she's left-handed."

"Upsets that applecart, doesn't it?" she said, her good humor restored.

He chuckled. "It's her right arm that's broken, which would still make it nigh impossible for her to drive. The truck's a standard shift."

She pushed with her foot to keep the swing in easy motion. "Can fingerprints tell you when they were put there?"

"Be nice if they could. We can extract prints that overlay each other. That shows the order, but not when." Walker drank up and set the empty mug on the table near him.

"Uncle Rod mentioned that Pattysue had filed two assault complaints on Morgan in the past. She was also heard saying that 'he just wants murdering.' From what little I know about him, that sounds about right." She finished her tepid coffee and made a face.

"Where'd you hear that?" CJ asked. Siam stood up, stretched, and head-butted CJ's hand. He stroked the cat the full length of his furry back.

"At that baby shower we went to, I overheard Birdie Mandrill telling a woman that someone at the emergency clinic had told her. Told Birdie, that is." She set her empty cup in the holder on the glider's arm.

Sheriff Walker Bainbridge huffed and cleared his throat. "More like Birdie dragged it out of that person. She could haul secrets out of the Pentagon, and they'd thank her for doing it. Wonder if she could use a job interrogating suspects? Someone like Birdie would be useful, if she could only keep her mouth shut when she was on the other side of the door." His words dripped with scornful sarcasm.

Maggie felt her cheeks grow hot. "Oh. I should consider the source then."

"Bob liked his booze, and he could turn plum ugly. Last time I saw him was a few days before he died, in the Rusty Anchor over on Camp Road. He had quite an edge-on that night." CJ said, his Southernisms mixing with Yankee-speak.

"He usually hung out at the Dipped Oar Bar, but maybe he'd worn out his welcome," CJ continued. "He'd gotten into a fight with the husband of one of his lovers. Lyle might have killed Bob if the bartender hadn't kicked them both out. Heard tell that Lyle was going to stay on the warpath until he could even the score."

"Well, CJ, under the circumstances, I wouldn't blame Pattysue," Maggie said. "Not with her child hurt, too. For saying that, I mean."

"Your presumptions about Morgan's vehicle are now evidence, Maggie. Thank you for pointing that oversight out to me," the sheriff said, without heat. "I had to call the State Police in on this because we don't have the resources locally. With this amount of evidence, it's become a homicide. The rules have changed." He shifted sideways on the pew and draped his arm across the back.

"The forensic team checked the truck over, as well as the surrounding ground where you showed us. I got the report back yesterday. The truck had been moved, jerked backwards quick and hard. Folks in these parts, who drive vehicles with standard transmissions, especially facing on a downward slope like his driveway has, often park in reverse and set the hand brake. His was in first gear and the brake wasn't set."

"And the scratches?" Maggie asked.

"Those scratches on the hood do match the paint found on Morgan's belt buckle. It appears that he rolled and then slid off the hood, just like you thought. His head hit a jagged chunk of rock, part of the old stonewall fence. The medical examiner said the rock knocked Morgan out and fractured his skull. The head trauma is what killed him."

"Did he die … instantly?"

The sheriff waited a space. "Could've."

Chills ran down Maggie's spine and she shivered.

"He was unconscious, Maggie. He never knew what

happened," CJ said, his voice soft with compassion.

Maggie sighed. "Like I said before, I don't know the kith and kin. Though I sure met enough people at my folks' party." She smiled at CJ, who grinned right back, emphasizing the dimple that made her heart do cartwheels.

"What I don't understand is, where did Morgan get all his money?" Maggie asked. "That truck, all chromed up, cost a bundle. Victor also seems to have hoards of money, and no visible source of income either. What if they were in cahoots, blackmailing somebody? If Morgan double-crossed Victor, he could have retaliated and done the deed."

"He's small enough. Using the truck as a weapon would suit him," the sheriff agreed.

"Furthermore, Victor grew up with my sisters − lucky him," she said, dripping sarcasm. "With his mother's devilish streak, too, he'd certainly know a bunch of practical jokes."

"It's all speculation, Maggie. No way to prove it," CJ said.

"No, other than challenging him just to hear what he'd say."

"I appreciate your assistance, Maggie, seriously. But stay away from Victor Turner, he's got questionable connections." Sheriff Bainbridge moved his stocky body off the bench and touched the brim of his hat. "Good coffee, too, thanks. Later!"

CJ unfolded his long frame from the confines of the Adirondack chair. He stood up and shifted the cat off his lap and into the chair. "There you go, Siam."

Siam batted CJ's hand as he ruffled the cat's ears.

"Be seein' you, Maggie." CJ tapped the dip of the front brim of his hat in a goodbye salutation.

"Aye, that you will," she said, returning his smile. *After I find Victor and have it out with him.*

32

Maggie Goes Sleuthing!

Wednesday, July 11th, early afternoon

MAGGIE PONDERED ONCE AGAIN where her hateful cousin got his money. He'd never held down a real job that she could remember. Victor's clothes were elegant, and he drove an expensive Lexus. Maybe he inherited money from one or another of his many wives? Time for a showdown − she'd had enough of his taunting, insinuations, and impractical jokes. Time to find some evidence, too, she hoped.

The sheriff had said that Victor was renting old man Watson's cabin on Blue Jay Lane, wherever *that* was. "Turn in right after the five mailboxes. It's the last one on the left, beside the big pine tree," may make sense to the locals who knew the area well, but Maggie had no idea where *any* nest of mailboxes might be in this town. She pulled the town map out of the drawer in the phone table. Blue Jay Lane veered off Henderson Road, several miles north of Loon Creek Road. It was one of several dead-end roads leading to Loon Creek.

Her aunt and uncle were off to an estate sale in Waterville. They had taken Larkin's Voyager. Maggie didn't dare drive their BMW, especially on what was likely a rough gravel road. She left a note on the peg where the keys had been hanging. Rod's Jeep smelled of gunpowder and Old Spice.

On the way north on Henderson Road, Maggie had time to think. Nervous, because she hated confrontations, but Victor had aggravated her one time too many. She wasn't about to back down. She was bigger than him and in far better shape.

Three roses. Long-stemmed roses were from a florist, not conveniently gathered from a wild rose bush. How long did it take roses to wither and die? That presumed premeditation.

The snake. Heaven knows there's no shortage of the slimy creatures. She couldn't tell one garden snake from another, and didn't want to. Neither did it leave a calling card for further identification.

One point in Victor's favor, though, was that he didn't like chocolate. He could have gotten the candy box from his mother, a girlfriend, or most anyone. The box was too common to be tracked back to the deed-doer.

Snap powder? Untraceable. Made up of common ingredients, easily obtained, CJ had told her. *Not* a comforting thought.

"What if he has a gun?" she said to the windshield. But she couldn't come up with a satisfactory answer to her own question. She was reconsidering confronting Victor when she found herself at the intersection of Blue Jay Lane.

Blue Jay Lane was nothing more than a narrow dirt track leading to the Creek. She was unlikely to find proof that Victor was behind the impractical jokes or Morgan's murder. She'd worked herself into a tizzy by now. Having come this far, she convinced herself to Just Do It and get it over with.

The cabins were small and terminally cute. Maggie wondered why Victor would rent here rather than a five-star hotel in a larger town. As she hit a deep pothole, she decided it had to be a matter of convenience, not elegance.

At the last cabin on Blue Jay Lane there was a pine tree, and no car in the driveway. Maybe Victor wasn't home. In one sense, Maggie was glad. In another, she was mad. She'd come here on a mission and was determined to finish it.

She stepped up onto the miniscule porch, opened the screen, and knocked on the front door. Music was coming from inside. Maybe he was home after all, so she pounded on the door. Was the little pipsqueak avoiding her?

Perturbed, she rattled the doorknob to get his attention. Bless the cranky old lock, the latch shifted and the door creaked open. From that excellent vantage point, she could see straight into the tiny bedroom. No one was home. With opportunity knocking, as she considered that pithy saying, she glanced over her shoulder before stepping into the cabin.

It was a simple floor plan with galley kitchen on the left, front room to the right. Bathroom and bedroom were at the back of the cabin, visible from where she stood just inside the door. No one was home except the field mouse that darted past her in a gray blur.

Modern rock music was coming from an old radio sitting on the kitchen counter. She turned it off. She walked to the bedroom, the ancient floorboards creaking their protest.

A double bed, a small armoire, and an antique three-drawer dresser were the only pieces of furniture in the room. The contents of the armoire were disappointing: just Victor's clothes. She approached the dresser and tried to pull out the shallow top drawer, but it wanted to stick. A hefty tug almost set Maggie on her education. The drawer didn't come all the way out, but it was out far enough.

The motion had unsettled a stack of silk handkerchiefs. Beside them was a set of pearl cufflinks. She picked up the one that was missing its pearl and examined it. It looked about the right size to accept the pearl she'd found in front of Bob Morgan's truck.

Oh, razzlefratz, I didn't think to bring gloves. Fine sleuth, I am. Oh, well.

As she put the cufflink back, she noticed the corner of something red peeking out from under the handkerchiefs.

"Hmmm, what's this?"

It was a slim red leather-covered notebook. After a quick glance toward the front door, she opened the book. At first glance, the lists seemed to make no sense.

Letters and numbers: *Sen AY, 5.6.00 5K@m; Jud RB, 4.21.01 2K@m; CAL -> RBM, 5.12.07 1C/2@w* ... The pages were full of similar notations, some dating back many years.

"Oh my heavens, he's blackmailing these people! A senator, judge, and ..."

A heavy thud on the porch brought her back to her perilous position, standing as big as you please in Victor's bedroom holding an incriminating book. She'd have no logical excuse for rifling his bureau drawer, and didn't want to confront him now, not under these circumstances. He always carried a gun. She set the book on top of the bureau and tried to shove the drawer closed. It balked then gave way with a groan.

Something scraped against the kitchen window. *Drat! The book!* She tried to open the drawer again, but it wouldn't budge. In desperation, she slid the book way under the bureau and ran out the front door without closing it behind her.

No Victor in sight yet, and she wasn't about to go looking for him now. She was on the way out on Blue Jay Lane when she saw Victor's Lexus making the turn. Rod's old hat was on the seat. She shoved it on her head, removed her glasses and set them in her lap, hoping Victor wouldn't recognize her, especially driving Rod's Jeep.

In the rearview mirror she saw Victor pull into the driveway of the cabin. She put her glasses back on and drove north on Henderson Road. She was almost to the intersection of Morrilton Road when she noticed his car coming up fast behind her. The traffic light was with her, but he didn't make it in time. There was no way she could outrun him, and she wasn't going to risk Rod's Jeep, regardless. She headed west on Morrilton Road and barreled into the parking lot of the Mercantile. Safety in numbers in a public parking lot, she hoped, as she got out of the Jeep on shaky legs.

Victor pulled up beside her and jumped out of his car.

"What were you doing in my cabin?" He stood with his arms parked on his scrawny hips.

"What's your problem, Victor? I just was out for a drive. Went up and down all the roads leading to Loon Creek. There are some pretty cabins out there."

"I don't believe you, Maggie. You're up to something," he interrupted.

The best defense was a blustering offense in this case, so

Maggie challenged him. "*Me*, Victor? I might ask *you* the same thing."

"What do you mean?" He spat on the ground and switched his chaw to the other cheek.

"You know exactly what I mean. Practical jokes that aren't funny – nasty ones."

"What *are* you talking about?" Victor scowled, looking confused.

"I want to know why you're harassing me, Victor. Dead roses. A slinky surprise in a candy box …"

Victor's eyes widened in surprise as he broke in, "Listen, Maggie. The phone call, yeah, I had Tony do that. I don't know nothin' about that other stuff. You're kidding me. That's juvenile. I can't be bothered with such petty stuff."

Victor's denial rang true. *Well, darn. Back to square one.*

33

Pattysue, Just Once More

Thursday, July 12th, morning

WITH BROKEN SHAKE SHINGLES, the window glass dull with rain spots and mud spatters, and peeling paint on the front door like green dandruff, the little cottage showed her years like a frowsy flower child – out of date and out of money. The shingled siding was painted white, but not recently. A twig wreath decorated with white buttons tied on with red wire was hanging on a rusty nail beside the front door, adding a defiant touch of whimsy.

Happy to be back at home, Pattysue was raging a one-armed war on cobwebs. Dust motes played leapfrog with dust bunnies, and a spider was weaving a new web in the corner. The dustpan and mop standing at parade rest against the sink gave mute testimony that broom warfare was imminent. She planned to make short work of the intruders. It was slow going with one arm in a cast, but she was determined to have her house clean once more. It might be shabby, but it would be shiny.

The phone's insistent summons interrupted her diligent attack on almost three weeks of neglect.

"Yes, we're home for good now, Sheriff. Anytime."

A few minutes later she heard Sheriff Bainbridge's car

pull into the gravel driveway and park. Pattysue met him at the screen door with a bottle of window cleaner tucked under her sling and a wad of dirty paper towels in her left hand.

They sat at her clean, scarred kitchen table. It was there in the cottage when the young Morgan family moved in. Straight out of the late forties, the top was pockmarked white metal. Around the dented edge, the red painted stripe was chipped. A matchbook under one leg kept the table from wobbling.

The sheriff took a deep drink of the iced tea she had given him on arrival. In her glass, the ice was melted. She hadn't bothered to refill it.

"Mrs. Morgan, did you drive yourself home from your sister's?"

"Please call me Pattysue, Sheriff. I'm no longer Mrs. Morgan," she said with calm insistence. "No, I can't drive yet. Carrie brought us home in my car. It'll be here when I can drive again. Coop followed us in his car."

Kaleen was under the table singing a lullaby. "Dolly's taking a nap. Shhh!" she admonished the adults. She wiggled out, cradling her baby doll.

Pattysue watched her daughter walk away. Kaleen swung the doll in a wide arc, singing in a squeaky voice, "*Rocky-bye baby in the treetops ... *"

"Bob's truck is gone. Did you take it?"

"We did. You'll get it back."

"I don't want it. Dump it in the lake or the Atlantic, for all I care. He loved that truck more than he did us," Pattysue said, unable to contain her anger.

"It's new. You might want to sell it."

"You're right," she conceded, "I may have to. We need the money."

"Where are his keys?"

"You've got the truck. Don't you have them? He always leaves, uh, left them in the ignition."

"That's pretty careless."

She glanced at him, wondering where he was going with the simple statements. "I thought so. It's a stupid thing to do, even in this little town." She stood up and brought the iced tea pitcher over to the table. After refilling both glasses, she sat down. "From the day he bought that truck, his keys have never passed that door."

"Did you ever drive it?"

"Are you kidding? That was *his* truck, period. He wasn't about to let any *woman* drive it, and certainly not *me*. They hired a woman mechanic at his favorite shop and he switched to another garage." She gestured with one hand as if dismissing the stupid egotism of certain men.

"When you went out together, did you go in his truck or your car?"

"His truck, of course. He wasn't about to drive my car, unless he absolutely had to, like taking it to the shop. He called it a beached sunfish." Pattysue pointed at the window. "You can see it from here."

It was an odd shade of yellow, faded and splotchy, with rust spots on the fenders. A tabby cat snoozed on the hood. In a flurry of blue feathers, a blue jay made a strafing run over the orange ball of fluff. The cat bolted toward the safety of the house and dove under the porch.

The sheriff smiled and turned back to Pattysue. "When

was the last time you two went out?"

"It was for Valentine's. We went to his parents' house in Camden for dinner." She started to take a drink and the ice shifted. Tea dribbled down her chin. She grabbed a paper towel to catch the drips.

"Where are your keys?"

She frowned at him as she wiped tea off her shirt. "What do you mean?"

"Your keys, keychain. May I see them?"

Pattysue went to her bedroom and returned with her purse. She thought for minute, then unzipped an inner pocket, fished out her keys, and laid them on the table. Pointing to each key in turn, she said, "My house key, car key, and the key to the book store. This one with Kaleen's image doesn't go to anything. It's a fake."

Seeing his questioning frown, she elaborated with a happy smile. "Kaleen gave it to me for Mother's Day. Bob was out of town, and Coop took her shopping."

"When was the last time you saw these keys?"

She wrinkled her brows, concentrating on the days following …

"Coop drove us in my car over to their house. Carrie followed in hers. The minute we parked, Coop handed me the keys. I zipped them in this inner pocket where they couldn't fall out."

"Did anyone, like Cooper or your sister, use your car while it was at their house?"

"No, only when Carrie brought us home yesterday."

"What about those keys?" He pointed to the key rack on the wall by the screen door.

"What? Oh, those must be Bob's keys, Sheriff. His has," she hesitated, "a key to the house, my car, his truck, and the camper."

She stared at her keys on the table and chewed on a ragged thumbnail. "If you've got the truck, what are his keys doing up there?"

"What keys did Carrie use?"

Pattysue thought back to yesterday's hustle and bustle. She and Kaleen were all packed and ready to go. Coop had taken his keys out of the tray by the door and opened the trunk of his car to load their suitcases. Right before they left, Carrie had picked up ...

"Those," she said, staring wide-eyed at the key rack.

"Where is Carrie now?"

"You just missed her." She glanced at the clock. "She dropped off these pictures about a half-hour ago."

"Are there any pictures of her in here?" He tapped the thick envelope.

Pattysue dumped it out and scuffed through the photos, displaying them in a ragged fan.

"This one, they're dressed up for their fifth anniversary dinner. And here's one of her playing with Kaleen at the pool in the park." She extracted the photos from the stack.

"These two will do fine. May I take them?" However polite, his tone brooked no argument. "And I want those keys, too."

He asked her for a small plastic bag. Using his pen as a carrier, he dropped the keys in. After writing a receipt for them, he put one copy inside and zipped the top closed.

Coming from the hallway a small voice scolded her dolly

for not drinking her milk.

"Is there something wrong, Sheriff?"

"You're fine."

"We were going next door to Mrs. Sanger's for lunch. Is that okay?"

"Even better."

34

Maggie Faces a Confrontation

Thursday, July 12th, mid-afternoon

MAGGIE DROPPED THE PHONE back in its base and ran upstairs for her purse.

Now, standing in the utility room, she checked the key rack. The keys to Larkin's van were the only ones left. Rod was off on some mission at the hardware store. Larkin was lunching with an old friend and had taken the BMW.

She wrote a quick note and stuck it on the empty peg.

The phone rang again. Maggie hesitated then ran to answer it.

"Oh, hi, CJ. Sorry, can't talk now. I've got to run. I just had a frantic call from Pattysue Morgan. Seems Kaleen's running a high fever and is awfully sick. Pattysue still can't drive. She needs me to take them to the emergency clinic. I'll talk to you when I get back."

A few minutes later, she pulled the van into Pattysue's driveway. Pattysue ran down the porch steps and intercepted Maggie before she got very far.

Pattysue was crying, unchecked tears streaming down her face. "M-Maggie, I'm sorry."

"Where's Kaleen?"

"They m-made me call you!"

"Who did?"

"We did." Victor stepped out from around the corner of the cottage.

A short woman, dressed in a white blouse, navy blue skirt, in full makeup, and an upswept hairstyle, came up behind him.

"Where's Kaleen?" Maggie repeated, grabbing Pattysue's arms.

"With Mrs. S-Sanger," Pattysue snuffled. "She's not sick."

Maggie let her go as Victor hurried closer.

"My little red book," Victor demanded. "I want it back now, Maggie. The one you stole."

"What book?" Maggie recalled the slim red volume she'd tossed under his bureau and hoped she could maintain a poker face. *Evidently not!*

Victor reached into his jacket and pulled out a gun. What kind, she didn't know. It was a moot point. Never having stared down the business end of a firearm before, it looked awfully big and captured her undivided attention.

"I won't say it again. I want my book back."

"Are you *deaf?* I don't have it, Victor."

He moved to Pattysue's right side and held the gun to her temple.

Pattysue whimpered and froze.

C'Anna stepped closer to Victor.

Maggie watched the woman's face dissolve from calm demeanor into absolute disgust. It was Carrie, dressed in her hostess uniform! She hoped Pattysue's big sister's protective instincts would kick in.

Carrie lunged forward, catching Victor from behind just as Pattysue brought her right arm up. Using her cast as a weapon, she knocked the gun out of Victor's hand. He started to move. Again using her cast, Pattysue struck him on the head. He was down for the count.

Carrie picked up the gun, swiveled, and aimed for Victor's head, but she stumbled. Maggie moved toward her. She turned the gun on Maggie.

Pattysue screamed, "Carrie! Don't!"

Distracted, Carrie jerked around to face her sister.

That's all Maggie needed. She hooked her leg behind Carrie's, shoved her gun arm up as she pushed Carrie and tipped her backwards.

She landed hard on the rough driveway, sputtering, the wind knocked out of her. The gun flew out of Carrie's hand. Victor moaned and sat up, rubbing his temple. Maggie kicked the gun far out of the reach of both miscreants.

Shaking with the adrenalin rush, she was never so happy to hear sirens and the sound of the sheriff's car pulling in behind her. When she heard the rumble of CJ's truck, she broke down.

* * * * *

The sheriff arrested Victor Turner and Carrie Larradeau and had them carted off to the county jail by two of his deputies.

Maggie, Pattysue, CJ, and Walker were sitting around Pattysue's kitchen table, rehashing the event.

"What alerted you?" Maggie asked CJ.

"I remembered seeing Pattysue and Kaleen at the

Mercantile this morning. That little girl was her typical bouncy self. Something didn't ring true, so I called Walker."

Sheriff Walker Bainbridge said, "I was about to find Carrie and haul her in for questioning when CJ called me. With you in the mix, I thought I'd better get here PDQ."

Maggie wasn't sure how to take his comment, so she let it go. "I'm so glad you did."

Pattysue looked at Maggie, with tears shining in her eyes. "I didn't want to call you. Carrie *made* me. She insisted that Victor promised to kill her, or me, if he didn't get some important book back from you. He was sure you stole it from his cabin. He wanted it back in the worst way. Carrie convinced me that you'd come here if Kaleen was seriously hurt."

"Quite true, and I did."

The sheriff cleared his throat. "What's this important book he's goin' on about, Maggie?"

"Blackmail. If you go to his cabin, his little red book is under the dresser."

"Maggie ..."

Maggie jumped in before the sheriff could fuss at her. "I went there in the first place to confront him about harassing me, Walker. He denied it, and for whatever reason, I believe him." She proceeded to tell him about the faulty old lock, the temptation to snoop since she was presented with the perfect opportunity, and the conversation with Victor afterward in the parking lot of the Mercantile.

The sheriff heaved himself up off the chair. "Maggie, I don't know what I'm going to do with you." He put on his hat.

"I need you to come up to the station and give a statement, Pattysue. I want to put that oily so-and-so behind bars. Tomorrow's fine, better, actually."

"I'll ask Mrs. Sanger to bring me in tomorrow, Sheriff. Thank you. But … what's going to happen to Carrie?"

"When you come in tomorrow, we'll have some answers for you then, too," he replied with kindness.

CJ took Maggie's hand. They said their goodbyes to Pattysue with hugs. She walked out with them since she was heading next door to collect her daughter.

Before closing the door of Larkin's van, CJ kissed Maggie. "I for one know what *I'm* going to do with you." He shut the door and strode toward his truck.

With that declaration playing havoc with her thoughts, Maggie drove back to Eagles' Rest.

35

Maggie Sees Pictures
Worth Many Tears

Thursday, July 12ᵗʰ, late afternoon

AT EAGLES' REST LATER THAT DAY, Maggie was looking through her aunt's old photo albums and scrapbooks, a pleasant, mindless activity appreciated after the earlier afternoon's high adventure. She was somewhat surprised to find many pictures of herself interspersed chronologically throughout the pages. CJ sat close beside her, his hand barely brushing her shoulder. It was very comfortable to have him there.

The rogue thought that he reminded her of someone surfaced every now and then. But was she putting too much into it? Attempting to peel back the pages of decades, hoping to find the young man he once was? *Fruitless exercise, no doubt. Time to give it up.* She was more content with the known quality of the man sitting right here beside her, than the nebulous, intangible dream of what might have been, but wasn't.

Siam, draped on the back of the loveseat, snuggled up against CJ's arm with one soft paw also resting on Maggie's shoulder.

Sheriff Walker Bainbridge strode into the Lake Room. "CJ?" With a jerk of his head, he motioned toward the breakfast room.

Maggie returned the scrapbook to its shelf and followed the men, stopping at the near end of the kitchen island. She leaned against it with arms folded, observing the group huddled around the table.

The sheriff laid the two pictures he'd taken from Pattysue earlier, on the table. CJ sat down across from his friend. Larkin came in, wiping her hands on her apron, and stood between her husband and the lawman.

"There was a couple sitting behind us at the Rusty Anchor last Saturday night, Walker," CJ said. "I couldn't see the woman's face. She was sitting with her back to us." Pointing to the man in the anniversary photo, he added, "But that looks like her companion, all right."

Peering over Walker's shoulder, Larkin said, "Her hair is styled in a different way here, but there's no disguising those eyes. That's C'Anna, the hostess at The Pennyroyal." She paused. "She was so attentive, remember, Rod? She kept peeking in on us although our waiter was efficiency itself."

"Ayuh. She shot Maggie a cold look when we first came in. I had no idea why. It was only a flash, but I saw it. Then we three got to visiting, and I forgot all about it. Pleasant company does that. Besides, the food there is exceptional and worth our undivided attention."

"What about this one?" Walker tapped on the pool scene photo.

"Those big glasses! She came with Pattysue to the baby shower. I do declare, for a woman as well endowed as that,

that bathing suit leaves little to the imagination," Larkin exclaimed, her tone indicating that her Southern lady sensibilities were offended.

Walker tapped the photo of the couple. "That's Mr. and Mrs. Cooper Larradeau. Dressed up, she wears contacts. In those big green glasses she looks a lot different. Carrie's maiden name is Caroline Anna Davidsby. She sometimes goes by C'Anna."

"She mothered her younger sister almost to the point of smothering the poor child. Very strong, is the mother instinct, and it doesn't have to be our own flesh and blood children for whom we have that affection." Larkin gazed into the middle distance.

"Since Coop had no use for Bob, Pattysue could visit with her sister only when Bob was out of town. The few times we saw the sisters together here in Baysinger Cove, Carrie was never dressed up, which is why we didn't recognize her at The Pennyroyal," Larkin added. "As Maggie mentioned, makeup can effectively disguise a person. Carrie's abundant freckles are non-existent in this fancy dress persona."

Rod scratched his head. "But that still doesn't address the question of who is plaguing Maggie."

"Victor Turner denies doing it, and Maggie believes him," the sheriff said.

Rod continued speculating. "It might have been Carrie, attempting to dissuade her from sleuthing, even though Maggie wasn't overly serious about it. She was right on the mark when we were playing Whodunit at the restaurant."

Sheba padded up to Maggie and whimpered, meaning

that she expected to be fed. Siam was close enough behind to be the dog's shadow. Maggie honored both of the fur kids' requests and left them to enjoy their snacks. After getting herself a glass of ice water, she joined the group in the breakfast room. She sat sideways on the window seat, hugging her knees to her chest.

Walker tapped on the image of the woman in the pool. "If I'd seen this, and what Deputy Capstone ferreted out from Morgan's truck, before I called Cooper Larradeau, it would have saved me an embarrassing phone call."

"How so?" Rod inquired.

"We found some fancy feminine underwear in the camper of Morgan's truck. They weren't Mrs. Morgan's, she's petite everywhere. They were sized more like her sister would wear. Deputy Capstone also found an empty gift box of expensive perfume. Wedged under the cot's mattress, he discovered a picture of a woman wearing those scanty garments. He met me at the station a little while ago and gave me the picture, and the results of his investigation."

"What about the jackknife and gum wrapper?" CJ asked.

"The knife was Morgan's. I almost dismissed the gum wrapper out of hand since half of the town's younger generation chews."

"Better a chew than a chaw," CJ said.

"Agreed." The big lawman leaned back. "But with murder, every little bit matters. I've learned not to discount anything. It'll all fit, sooner or later. We ran the prints from inside the camper, the cab, the door, and even the gum wrapper. We got a match. They are all Carrie's prints."

"How do you happen to have her prints on file?" Rod

asked. "Does she have a record?"

Speaking up for the first time in over an hour, Maggie said, "Mine are on file, too."

"You what?" CJ blustered.

"Nothing criminal." She unfolded her legs and swung herself around on the bench seat to face the table. "Third grade, my whole class was fingerprinted."

"Carrie's file isn't quite so innocent. When she was eighteen, she worked for Victor Turner as a high-dollar escort in Portland."

"We all know what *that* means," Maggie said.

"I called Cooper Larradeau and asked for his wife's legal name, where she works, and what size bra she wears. Let me tell you, that was one uncomfortable conversation. I like Coop. I went to school with his dad. I've known his family for years. After we talked, I think Coop realized his wife was in serious trouble."

"Does Coop know about her record? And that she may have murdered Bob?" Maggie asked.

"Doubt it. But he soon will," the lawman replied.

"Poor Cooper and poor Pattysue, too," Larkin sympathized. "Is she aware that her sister was dawdling in the gazebo with her husband?"

Maggie snickered at her aunt's uncharacteristic disregard for flying pronouns.

The sheriff grinned and winked at Maggie. "Not yet, Larkin, but Pattysue suspects something. She's just young, not dumb. She's had a rough couple of weeks. I discovered Morgan's truck keys on the key rack in her kitchen. Pattysue remembered that Carrie had put them there."

"Pattysue announced she was filing for divorce, so Carrie must have panicked. She'd alienate Pattysue and most likely lose Cooper. If she could silence Morgan, she would be out a lover, but everything else would be as it was," Larkin replied, wrinkling her patrician nose, pronouns now back in place.

Maggie decided to add her own observations to this discussion. "When C'Anna in her hostess persona stood behind Victor, it took me a second before I realized that she was Carrie. I hoped she would try to protect Pattysue, and she did. It was bad enough that Victor pulled a gun on me but when she did … I'd had enough. I'm glad it's over and done, bar the shouting."

Larkin leaned over and kissed Maggie's forehead. Maggie stood up and headed for the kitchen. A few minutes later, she returned with a plate stacked with chocolate chip cookies. She sat down next to CJ, who didn't hesitate to pick up two cookies and a napkin from the basket on the table.

Before leaving Pattysue's home, Sheriff Bainbridge had dispatched two deputies to take both Carrie Larradeau and Victor Turner to the county jail for questioning. The diabolical pair had been put in separate interrogation rooms and left to cool their heels while the sheriff questioned his friends here at Eagle's Rest.

The musical theme from the "Lone Ranger" burst into the silence. Walker retreated to the Lake Room to take the call.

Storming back to the breakfast room, he announced, "Jobina Court is dead. She didn't answer when her mother called her to lunch. Her father found her. It appears she was poisoned."

"Carrie may be a double dipper!" Maggie exclaimed, sitting bolt upright.

"I suspect you're right. We'll soon find out. We're waiting on Cooper and a lawyer to get to the jail."

"Why include her husband? I thought spouses weren't allowed in the interrogation room," Rod asked.

The sheriff replied, "Not as a rule. I want him there because as Carrie's husband, he has an emotional investment in finding out the truth. He might add facts to corroborate or contradict Carrie's story. If Carrie lies, he would be more apt to catch her in it."

"Interesting." Rod dusted cookie crumbs off his fingers.

Setting her half-eaten cookie on a napkin, Maggie expounded on her reasons and logic for suspecting Carrie. "Killing Morgan, I think was an opportunity taken, premeditated in the sense that Carrie was determined to do something to stop this blight on her sister's life. Stalking Morgan, maybe on the pretext of a tryst, she found him soused to the gills, saw a chance, and took it. Her mistake was in pocketing the keys. Habit gets you every time. That's one piece of the puzzle I missed. You caught it, Walker."

"What about the pearl you found, the one that I gave you grief over?" the sheriff asked.

"The pearl is hers, too, I'll bet," Maggie replied. "Though I had hoped it was the one missing from Victor's cufflink. Anyway, at the baby shower, I complimented Pattysue on her necklace. It was an exquisite cultured pearl drop. She and her sister had twin necklaces. Carrie wasn't wearing hers. I was distracted right then by meeting an old friend.

"The incident stuck in my mind. How I'd use that for a plot line in a book. And at The Pennyroyal, all gussied up, I certainly didn't recognize her. Even her speech patterns were different. It was as if she were two completely different women. Her nameplate said 'C'Anna,' and I didn't make the full connection then. She shot me a look that was right poisonous, but it happened so fast I thought I was seeing things. Super-active imagination, you know."

Walker smoothed down his handlebar moustache in the manner of a man wondering if he'd show up in a book someday.

"Guess I didn't do so well sleuthing," she said with a resigned sigh.

"You almost got it. With what little you had to go on, Maggie, you did fine. You didn't know where his keys ended up, for one. But your instincts were right on target. You'll get better with practice. Maybe next time."

"Practice? *Next* time?" she yelped. "I promise you, Walker, I'd just as soon do my sleuthing vicariously, curled up in an easy chair with a cat, chocolates, and a cozy. To be a real-time amateur detective, I'm a very reluctant one," Maggie added with her usual spunk.

Siam head-butted Maggie's leg, and she reached down to pet him. Being contrary, he batted her hand then took off in a streak of silver gray fur to bedevil Sheba.

"A sideline gumshoe, eh?" Walker chuckled, then sobered. "We did another background check on Turner, since he showed up at the funeral. True to tradition, it's an odd bunch that attends funerals. Running an in-depth check on

Morgan as well, we found a connection. They have had strange business dealings for many years, including blackmail. Most recently, Turner and Morgan were involved in a shady deal with one of the marinas in a town west of here, and there's suspicious activity in several other places where their names came up together."

"Even our little village gets a whiff of eau-de-Mafia every so often, right?" Maggie asked.

"Unfortunately, yes. Can't seem to get away from it anywhere," CJ concurred.

The sheriff cleared his throat. "I'll get a search warrant for Victor Turner's cabin. Now, where'd you say you tossed his little red book, Maggie?"

"It's way under the dresser. And before you ask, my prints will be on it since I did not wear gloves."

"I suspected as much."

"I had *so* hoped the pearl was Victor's," Maggie repeated with a wistful sigh.

"Sorry to disappoint you," the sheriff said after polishing off his third cookie. "Victor Turner has an unimpeachable alibi. He was in the company of several Federal officers for about thirty-six hours, a timeframe overlapping the time of Morgan's death."

"Oh, well. I cannot stand that man, and I'm not *his* favorite cousin either," she said with conviction. She tapped her bottom lip, lost in concentration, connecting the dots.

After a long minute, she said, "I believe Victor isn't the one playing the non-funny jokes. They are too subtle for him. And he did deny it. It may have been Carrie, trying to scare me off. Other than spooky, frightening, and distasteful, none of it was physically harmful."

"Anyone else in your family who could be upset about your position here?" the sheriff asked.

"Referring to my getting reacquainted with relatives from whom I should never have been separated?" she asked. *I wonder why it has taken me so long to find my way back.*

She glanced up in time to catch the look shared between her aunt and uncle. Thinking hard for several minutes, she recalled an earlier conversation with Larkin.

"Well, there are three younger sisters. We haven't heard anything from them in years, decades even. Regardless, I don't think there's any reason for them to be in the picture now."

"Why not?"

"Never was any love lost between us. Beryl, the oldest of the trio, hated me. The feeling was mutual. Amber, two years younger than Beryl, was antagonistic. Ruby, the baby, was ambivalent. Revenge? What for? Money? I wrote them out of my will and my life a long time ago. My so-called sisters are all old history. Shouldn't matter a whit now."

Sheba padded over and leaned against Maggie's leg. She reached down, and Sheba stuck her cold nose in Maggie's palm.

"Furthermore, on Sunday morning I'll be winging my way back to Oklahoma. When I'm gone, so will the trouble be also."

Walker Bainbridge answered his cell phone. Rising to leave, he put on his hat, gathered up his papers and photos. "I need to meet my deputy at the jail. Thank you, Maggie, for your insight. If I don't see you again before you leave, travel safe. And don't you be a stranger in Baysinger Cove. Later, Rod and Larkin, CJ."

36

Carrie, It's a Done Deal

Thursday, July 12th, early evening

IN THE INDUSTRIAL GRAY-PAINTED interrogation room at the Baywater County jail, Caroline Anna Larradeau, dressed in her crumpled Pennyroyal hostess uniform, was sitting as if her backbone was starched like her blouse. She sat with her hands in her lap, worrying a hangnail.

Her husband sat in the chair at her right. Cooper's brother, Jason Larradeau, in the chair on her left, was acting as her temporary legal counsel.

Seated at the other side of the scarred wood table were Sheriff Walker Bainbridge and his two deputies.

Sheriff Bainbridge stood up. Using a remote control, he turned on a sophisticated audio/visual recording device mounted in the upper corner of the room. For the record, he stated the date and time, named the persons present, and their reasons for being there. He pocketed the remote and sat down in the chair at the end of the table nearest the door, placing him nearer Carrie.

He was closer to her than she liked him to be.

Carrie was Mirandized for the second time. "Yes, I understand," she said, willing her voice not to shake.

"Pattysue said you forced her to call Maggie and set her

up. Why?"

Maybe now's my chance to get back at Victor, that slimy toad.

"Victor Turner called me. Seems he's got a very important book that came up missing. He was sure Maggie took it. He ordered me to call Maggie on some trumped up excuse to get her out somewhere alone. That was stupid. Maggie doesn't know me, and she's not that dumb. So he tells me to call Pattysue and come up with something. He wanted his book back immediately. Didn't care how I went about it, but I had to get the book for him. He said if I valued my life, or my sister's, I'd do it. He would have killed us both, I'm sure of it."

"Do you know what was in this book?"

"Some men carry little black books. His book was red, for blood. Blackmail. He kept track of names, dates, and details. Bleeding people, a little bit at a time."

"Where were you Tuesday evening, June twenty-six?" the sheriff asked, leaning forward in his chair with his arm on the table.

The subject was an abrupt change, but she had expected that question. "Here in Baysinger Cove."

"Why?"

"My sister needed some more stuff." She shifted in the uncomfortable chair, wondering how this would all play out.

Cooper stiffened, but remained quiet.

"Did you go there to meet Robert Morgan?" The sheriff tapped his pen on the table. Tap-tap-tap.

She shifted in her chair again. Staring at the hard edge of the table, she snapped, "I didn't *meet* him."

Tap-tap-tap.

God, I wish he'd stop the darn tapping. It's drivin' me crazy.

For the space of a few seconds no one spoke or moved.

The sheriff tossed a baggie on the table. It slid and stopped a few inches away from her.

"Recognize them?"

Carrie froze.

"Whose are these?" he asked.

"Uh, Pattysue's."

"Look again."

She leaned forward. With an unsteady hand, she prodded one of the keys. "Oh, these are Bob's," she said, more confident now. "The one with the pin-up girl image is his camper key."

"How do you know that?"

"Pattysue told me." She shrunk a little bit down in her chair at the slight upturn of the pronoun, almost making the statement a question. *Maybe the sheriff didn't catch that.*

Tap-tap-tap.

"Did you kill Robert Morgan?"

She stared at the keys for a long minute then covered her face with both hands. *The keys! I hung them up in Pattysue's kitchen! I'm dead sunk now.* She dropped her hands. With a tortured sigh, she gave up. She started talking like she had just learned how to and couldn't stop.

"It was his own fault."

Jason Larradeau started to speak. She shushed the lawyer.

"Why'd I go there, Sheriff? Oh, it goes back a long ways.

Bob Morgan said he'd tell my story to Coop and Pattysue. He demanded money." She stared at the keys. "So, I paid him. I had to or—"

"Blackmail, Carrie?" Cooper interjected, shaking his head. "No way. That's impossible, Sheriff. I handle our finances. I'd know if there were any large debits."

Carrie turned to him. "The checks were made out to 'cash.' You never questioned those."

"No. I trusted you."

"Morgan got greedy. He wanted more money, more often. I knew sometime he'd get stinking drunk and brag. I couldn't come up with any more money," she moaned.

"So *kindhearted* Bob," her mouth curled in a feral sneer, "came up with an alternate plan. No cash? No problem! He'd just take it out 'in trade.' He demanded that I give him the works, and often. He told me in a nasty way not to be *shy* since I was so *well experienced*. He expected extra action, very steamy." She rung her hands together and cringed. "I hated every minute of it. He was Pattysue's *husband*, for heaven's sake!"

"Where and when was this, Carrie?" Cooper stared at her, wide-eyed, his lips parted, running a hand through his sandy brown hair.

"Sunday night, in the camper. Afterwards, I was in an awful hurry to get out of there. I grabbed my clothes but couldn't find my underwear. I didn't really care then, Coop. I just wanted *out* of there."

"What did Morgan have on you? What could he use for blackmail?" the sheriff asked. He beat a soft tattoo, tapping his pen on the manila folder there on the table in front of him. Tap-tap-tap.

Carrie worried her lower lip with her teeth. She suspected what was in that file. "Oh, brother, a lot." She crossed her arms and bent forward as if in pain, then rushed the next words. "Victor Turner and I were married right after he became business partners with Bob Morgan."

"What? That can't be true! You never told me you had been married before." Cooper's eyebrows collided in the middle of a scowl as fierce as a summer thundercloud presaging a hurricane.

She sat up, turned, and grasped his hand in both of hers. "No, Coop, it's true," she said, willing him to understand. "I had just turned eighteen. I had plans for a better life than a two-bit town would give me. Victor had money. He knew important people … so I married him. Two months later I wanted out. Victor wouldn't give me a divorce unless I agreed to work for two years as one of his high-dollar call girls in Portland. He made me sign a contract. I hoped he'd honor it. He did, but he never, ever, let me forget. I was scared to death that it would come back to bite me in the butt. Bob Morgan didn't forget it either." She paused and swallowed hard. Her voice full of disgust, she said, "He was my first and most frequent customer."

She looked up at her husband's stricken face. "Those two years were the worst kind of hell. I cannot tell you the *whole* story."

Cooper jerked his hand away and stared at her like he didn't know her, and curled his lip as if he didn't want to any longer.

"I left Portland the minute that contract ended. I moved

back here, hoping to wash the stink off me. I talked my way into a nice job at The Pennyroyal. I'd been working there for a couple of years when one day Coop came in with his parents. It was their thirtieth wedding anniversary dinner. A year later we were married."

Cooper slumped forward, staring at the floor. He folded his hands prayer fashion between his knees.

"It didn't take Bob long to find out Pattysue was my sister. He figured out a way to meet her. Charmed her, got her pregnant so he could do the 'right thing' by her." Her fingers made air quotes. "He married her just so's he could keep close tabs on me. He thought he'd hit the jackpot. It was a perfect setup, him being part of the family and all. Except that Coop wanted no truck with him, which messed up Bob's plans. Bob went too far with Pattysue this time, hurting her and Kaleen, too." She bounced her knee, her shoes making a hollow tap-tap on the cement floor.

"That's old news. Anyway, he called, insisting that I meet him that Tuesday night. He ordered me to talk Pattysue out of leaving him. He demanded another late-night rodeo in the camper. I did not keep our *date*." She stopped jiggling.

"Were you with Morgan that Tuesday night?" The sheriff threw the question at her.

She twisted her wedding ring round and round and round. "I wasn't *with* him."

"Your fingerprints are all over Morgan's truck," the senior deputy added.

I can't answer that. I've already said too darn much.

After a long moment, the sheriff threw out another question. "Jobina Court?"

This new tack surprised Carrie. "What about her? Nutcase."

Deputy Spencer spoke up. "We showed your picture to Rosemary at Rosie's Posies."

"So? I always get flowers there."

"Rosemary identified your picture, described your curt manner, and gave us every detail of the basket you ordered on Saturday, and the added candy," Deputy Spencer replied. "It matched the one we found near the victim."

Carrie sat rigid in her chair, her face immobile.

"Did you murder Jobina Court?" the sheriff demanded.

"Jobina's dead? Really?" Carrie smiled. "She was worse than a dog with a bone. She must have seen me with Bob. When did she die?"

"Today," the sheriff replied.

"Jobina finally ate that one special candy, huh? Took her long enough to get to it. Perfect. It's belated justice for James … and the babies. Saturday was the anniversary of her husband's drowning. Did you know that?" Her voice sounded far away, with a note of wonder attached to the question.

"Babies? Plural?" Cooper asked. His whole body slumped. He centered his elbows on his knees and put his head between his hands.

Coop's reaction brought her back to the present. "Jobina smothered her little girl, I know she did. She killed James, too." Her next words broke on a sob that came from the depth of her being. "Jealous and evil, mad Cousin Jobina. James was my high school sweetheart. Jay and I were going to marry right after graduation. But Jobina took him away from me. My sweet Jaybird, dead, and she killed him. I miscarried our baby … it was her fault …" she trailed off, caught up in the midst of a sad memory.

Cooper jerked upright. She turned to her husband and said in a low voice, "You never knew my full story. Now you see why I couldn't tell you I'd been married before, Coop?" She reached for him again, and he recoiled.

"Why, Carrie?" he moaned. "Why? Why couldn't you trust me? If you'd come to me first, I would have helped you…"

"For Pattysue. For you, for me," she interrupted, pleading, both hands wide apart in entreaty. "To save us, I *had* to betray you and my sister. I hated Bob Morgan. I wanted to keep you from knowing about it, to keep his filth away from you. I didn't set out to kill him."

Then her voice hardened. "But I ain't sorry the bastard's dead."

Like a chameleon, Carrie shifted moods. With heavy tears making rivulets down her no longer perfectly made-up face, she whispered, "I'm sorry, Cooper. I really am. I'm sorry I hurt you and Pattysue." She sniffed and pulled a tissue out of the box on the table. She blew her nose then slumped down like her backbone had turned from starch to wax.

"I would have taken care of Victor, too, if Maggie hadn't interfered. He intended to get in on Bob's blackmail scheme. I couldn't go back to that life, not ever."

She touched Cooper's arm. He leaped up, tipping over his chair. The action brought the sheriff out of his chair to stand beside Cooper.

Cooper's voice shook. "Only by the grace of God can I forgive you, Carrie, and I will. Not that you deserve *my* forgiveness, but so I can have peace." His voice stiffened into cold resolve. "Forgive your *actions*, no. Adultery, maybe, eventually I'd get over it. Murder? No. I cannot condone willful murder."

"But Coop, I tried to save us! You, my sister … and me."

"Two people are dead, and a third one you wish you could have taken care of? No, Carrie, hell, no. I am no longer your husband. I can't be, and won't be, married to a murderess."

Carrie sat back as if Cooper had struck her a physical blow. She watched her world dissolve around her.

Cooper turned to his brother. "Jason? Let's talk."

37

Maggie, *Vaya con Dios*

Saturday, July 14ᵗʰ, early evening

A CLASSIC KRIS KRISTOFFERSON SONG bespeaks the sadness of a Sunday morning coming down. Although today was Saturday, Maggie related wholly to the sentiment since she would be winging her way homeward on a Sunday. Tomorrow.

Thursday, Carrie Larradeau had been arrested for the murders of Bob Morgan and Jobina Court. Cooper Larradeau refused to be married to a murderess and was filing for divorce.

Victor Turner was arrested, as well, for blackmail and a host of other charges that Maggie couldn't keep straight. It was sufficient to the moment that he would be in jail for a long time, too.

Pattysue Morgan and her daughter were back at home, adjusting to the welcome peace of no drunken husband/father to fear. Over time, she would come to terms with her sister's duplicity.

This morning, Larkin had mentioned that Pattysue had accepted a dinner date for next Friday with the handsome Dr. Roy Grayson.

Maggie had found the welcome love of family. Possibly

a new romance, as well. A long-distance one, but she and CJ would manage. They were mature adults, not love-struck teenagers.

She was glad to be leaving with the knowledge that for some of the people in this saga, there was a happy ending.

At midday, they had dropped in at the Sawmill Hill Cafe for a quick lunch. Afterward, they stopped by May Flowers for a floral arrangement Larkin had ordered for the *Vaya con Dios* dinner this evening.

"Just the four of us, but we are dressing for dinner," she had informed everyone that morning.

The four of us! God bless her little matchmaking heart! Maggie smiled. She was enjoying the love and caring of her doting relatives. She would miss them so very much, she realized with a burst of enlightenment. To her, two of the most comforting and sweet words in the Bible were: *"But God ..."* He had faithfully answered one of her prayers: family. Her one regret was in leaving them behind. Oh, she knew that promises of future visits and more frequent calls would either belay the homesickness or sway her decision whether to stay in Oklahoma or return to Maine.

The housekeeper had been in yesterday, making the house totally ship-shape. Stella, of Stellar Bakery fame, was catering tonight's dinner. Kasha from Sweet Things was in charge of the dessert. Both ladies had insisted on serving and doing the after-dinner clean up, thereby relieving Larkin to fully enjoy the evening.

A white Irish lace tablecloth, a fifty-odd-year ago wedding gift from Larkin's mother, dressed the round oak dining room table. A low bouquet of red roses, baby's breath, tiny orchids, and gold spirals arranged in a black lacquer bowl, sat in the center, flanked by four white candles in silver candlesticks. Her grandmother's delicate china complimented the beautiful lace, and her vintage silverware, polished for the occasion, glowed in the soft candlelight.

Holding hands around the table, her uncle said grace. It was a prayer from the heart.

"Now, there's to be no more talk about murder or mayhem," Larkin insisted. "A genteel evening with pleasant conversation is highly preferable." She laid a snowy white linen napkin in her lap while Stella and Kasha delivered their dinner plates.

The candlelight did magical things to Larkin's pixie-cut white hair. Her heart-shaped face seemed to be wreathed in angel wings. Her ecru lace gown had a deep, artistically draped collar, accented by an Art Deco pin comprised of a large marquise-cut emerald surrounded by diamonds. The design was straight out of the Roaring Twenties and probably of that vintage, thanks to Larkin's years in the antique business, Maggie surmised.

After dinner, they indulged in the sumptuous dessert, Kasha's famous Chocolate Sin-Cinn Delight cake.

"Now we will retire to the Lake Room for a postprandial glass of wine," Larkin announced.

"Thank you for dinner, Auntie. This evening, well, you have made it so lovely, so special."

CJ stood up and held Maggie's chair for her, like the Southern gentleman he was.

"The evening is still before us, my dear, so let's enjoy it," Larkin said as Rod likewise assisted her.

Larkin placed the floral arrangement that had graced the dinner table on the low coffee table between the two loveseats in the Lake Room. A cranberry cut-glass ashtray held an assortment of guitar picks.

CJ sat beside Maggie with his arm across the back of the loveseat, his hand resting in a proprietary manner on her shoulder.

Sheba was asleep by Maggie's feet. Siam slumped, half asleep, over the edge of Sheba's basket.

"So, CJ, what are your plans for next week. Travel?" Rod asked.

"Yes. I'm off to Oklahoma City for a photography conference."

Maggie looked at him in surprise.

CJ smiled at her. "My original plan was to leave on Monday, but I rebooked my flight yesterday. If you don't mind, Rod, and you've no objections, Maggie, we can go to the airport together since we're on the same flight."

She mumbled what Yankees often say when they don't know what else to say, "I guess."

A few minutes later she said to her uncle, "That would save you a long day tomorrow. Good-bye days are always longer. And harder." She swallowed and blinked back a tear that was singularly determined to ruin her mascara.

"Still going home tomorrow, eh, Maggie? You sure you won't change your mind at the last minute, leave CJ at the airport and come running back to Baysinger Cove?"

Without waiting for her answer, Rod reached for a guitar pick and moved over by the piano. He picked up the six-string Guild, pulled a small stool out from under the piano's belly, and sat down. Siam jumped out of the basket and rubbed against Rod's legs.

After the first few notes, Maggie walked toward him and exclaimed, "That's *Struttin' the Blues*! Mike Auldridge." She stood beside him. "This is good stuff."

"I'm pleased that you know your blues and bluegrass," he said, switching to *Wayfaring Stranger*. In a strong baritone he began to sing the old folksong.

Maggie cocked her head like an attentive spaniel and sang the upper harmony in her soft contralto. When they finished the song, she pointed to the twelve-string Ovation. "May I?"

"Didn't know you still played, Maggie. Of course you may."

She perched on the piano bench and placed the round-backed guitar in her lap. After running through a few chords to get the feel of this unfamiliar instrument, she began the opening chords of *I'm So Lonesome I Could Cry*, classic Hank Williams. She closed her eyes and sang the haunting melody, every minor chord made personal.

"M'dear, that's beautiful. Do you remember your first guitar?" Rod asked when the notes of the last chord faded.

"You bet I do. It was my fourteenth birthday. You and Aunt Larkin were there for my party. You so surprised me with an acoustical guitar of my very own! I was thrilled. I still have it, as well as a twelve-string Ovation. It's not as upscale as this one. Someday I'll have a Guild like yours, Uncle."

"More'n likely," he replied. "What do you like to play?"

"I cut my musical teeth on the likes of Bob Dylan, Joan

Bayez, and the Serendipity Singers. My favorites back then were anything folk, or sung by Peter, Paul, and Mary. The first song I learned to play was *Blowin' in the Wind.* I like most country songs, and Southern gospel, of course. The old folk songs are the best. Maybe you'll remember this one."

Using the tips of her fingernails, she began picking out the opening chords of *Cruel War*, one of the sixties' most poignant protest songs. When she finished singing, CJ was standing next to her, staring at her face.

Uncomfortable with his close inspection, she attempted to diffuse the moment by rubbing the fingertips of her left hand with her thumb. "I haven't played for a while and these little bitties are vocal about it. Thank you, Uncle Rod, that was wonderful."

She wiped the guitar's neck with the chamois cloth then seated the beautiful instrument in its stand. Leaning over, she kissed her uncle's cheek. The fine wrinkles and creases were as soft as an old leather coat.

Eager for attention, Sheba scooted next to Maggie, putting in a bid for a good ear scratch session. If the dog could have purred, she would have.

Returning to the loveseats, Rod and Maggie each picked up a glass of wine that Larkin had poured during the musical interlude. The napkin-wrapped bottle rested in a heavy crystal vase.

Siam was taking care of the harmonious purring issue, parked in Larkin's lap.

"Yes, tomorrow, back to wind-across-the-plains Oklahoma, 'fraid so," she said, stoic to the end. "The most treasured thing I'm taking with me is the knowledge that I am a real part of this family. I promise to keep the distance between phone calls and visits much shorter."

Larkin answered with a rueful smile on her finely etched face. "Because in the early years we traveled so much, our correspondence was intermittent at best. We are better at it, now that we are settled."

"You still always remembered me at the important holidays. When I was eleven, Uncle Rod, you gave me a fashion doll and told me to design clothes for it. How you saw a clothing designer in me, without being around very often, always amazed me. That gift was not dismissed as naught. This dress is my own creation, thanks to your insight."

A long, full-square skirt of black lace set on point, overlaid an iridescent black silk taffeta underskirt trimmed in wide black Venice lace, creating a double handkerchief hem. The princess bodice and three-quarter length cape sleeves were silk-lined lace, trimmed with silk velvet ribbon.

Gratified smiles crinkled up the old man's face. The guitar pick made a soft plink as it hit the ashtray.

"Most charming, and becoming, Maggie dear. You wear black well. Not many women can, though so many do," Larkin said, her sniff conveying that her fashion sensibilities were assaulted at the very thought.

Stella and Kasha interrupted to thank the Richardsons and bid everyone a good night. Larkin locked the front door behind them.

"What about over the Christmas holidays? Can you get away at all then?" Rod asked.

CJ rejoined Maggie, and Larkin returned to sit beside her

husband.

Maggie sat back and just a wee bit closer to CJ, if that were possible without landing in his lap. "Quite tight then, time wise. It's the typical year-end madness since everyone wants to get a head start on the new year's to-do list. That's when our clients want their annual newsletters written yesterday. Those are ego driven, believe you me. Some folks are hard put to even write a grocery list, so they are in dire need of a ghostwriter." She paused, thought for a minute, and made up her mind. "When I get back in my office I'll up the deadline and clear the calendar."

"Excellent. That will be wonderful, Maggie. How much vacation time do you have remaining?" Larkin asked, beaming.

"This leave of absence didn't affect any of the vacation time I have accrued on my own merit. For the last two years I haven't taken very much time off. I still have five weeks coming, plus the holidays. You're sure now, that you want my company again so soon?" Maggie asked, feeling like she was four years old all over again.

"Child, you do not have to ask," Larkin scolded, though her tone was kind. "It's a given. I'll make the New Year's Eve Gala reservations Monday for the four of us. The lodge books up early."

Passing glasses of wine, CJ winked at Maggie. Dressed in a Western dinner jacket, he looked, well, simply dashing.

Rod glanced at his wife then turned to address Maggie. He ran his gnarled hand down across his mouth and chin, leaned forward on the loveseat and looked at her.

Wondering what this was all about, and unsure of what

251

was coming, she leaned forward as well, in essence meeting him halfway. With her elbow propped on one knee, she tapped her lower lip with her index finger.

"Maggie, when you come to the point in your life, when you've had enough of the madding crowd, you can come home to us. This *is* your home now. Believe it. Whatever happens, Larkin and I will back you up, spiritually, emotionally, financially."

Dropping both hands down in her lap, Maggie listened, her breath light and slow.

"If you want to start a business here, Larkin and I are willing to help you. We will be silent partners, if that will assist in achieving your dream, and will sit better with your independent spirit. Or we will take more active roles. Your call."

Searching into the depths of her uncle's jade green eyes, she saw love, honesty, and acceptance reflected there. She clasped her hands, prayer fashion. CJ laid his hand on her ramrod-stiff back. Through his touch, she knew that he was there for her as well.

She paced her words, speaking just above a whisper. "When I come ... home, I'll stand on my own. If ever I falter, I promise ... I promise I will ask for your help. Okay?"

"We were there the day you learned to walk, m'dear. We saw the look of surprise, wonder, and joy on your little face. Ever since that moment, you have been stubbornly determined to stand on your own two feet."

With a rueful nod at the truth in his words, she said, "I may come home sooner than we think." She groped through the voluminous skirt, searching for the now-elusive pocket hiding her hankie. CJ slipped his from his jacket pocket and gave it to her. She took it gratefully, mopping her tear-streaked face.

"Dear child, it's all yours, whether you take it now, or later," Larkin added, without clarifying the statement.

"What do you mean?" she asked, alert to nuances.

CJ refilled her glass of wine.

This stuff is good. Um ... was this the second, or third glass? Oops! With the high emotion cleaving the air, I might just have another one.

"Maggie, m'dear, Larkin and I are not getting any younger, to coin a hackneyed phrase. We had no children together. I am a wealthy man and Larkin is in no mean street herself, praise God. We love you as our own. And to that end, Maggie, other than a few minimal bequests, you are our sole inheritor."

For one of the few times in her life, Maggie was rendered speechless. *Oh, turtlefeathers, just bring the bottle!*

38

Maggie Has a Revelation

Saturday, July 14th, late evening

A CARD-CARRYING MEMBER of the technologically challenged populace, after lessons under her uncle's patient tutelage, Maggie had mastered enough of the complexities of his stereo system to use the CD player. She selected Conway Twitty, Charlie Rich, and the Righteous Brothers CDs, and slipped them into the disc changer.

Her doting aunt and uncle had said their goodnights and retired to their bedroom, leaving the lovers, Larkin intimated, time alone.

This vacation was supposed to be a rest?

Maggie walked over to the bookcase wall. On one of the lower shelves of the bookcase, she was surprised to find her high school yearbooks tucked in with other historical titles. *Historical? I'm not that old – or am I? Um, probably.*

There she was, on a satiny page of Hall-Dale High School's "Venture" yearbook. She had a timeless hairstyle of long, wavy black hair, and long bangs hovering above her eyebrows. A half-smile that didn't reach her eyes showed her just as suspicious of the camera then as she had been in kindergarten. *Was I ever this impossibly young? Seventeen. Just a puppy!* With realistic acknowledgement of the ever-widening gap between Then and Now, she began to close the annual but CJ took it from her.

"Harlan? Somehow I thought you were a Richardson." He looked distracted and thoughtful as he took the book from her. He looked at the page again before replacing it on the shelf. "Maggie Storm Harlan."

He spoke so low that she almost missed hearing what he said before she answered his question. "I am a Richardson on the distaff side. Marion Richardson Harlan was my mother. She was uncle Rod's younger sister," she said, distracted by another slim volume on the shelf. She pulled out Belgrade High School's yearbook, "The Echo."

She had attended BHS in her freshman year, after which she and her grandparents had moved to Hallowell for her remaining three years of high school. She turned the pages, stopping to read some of the full-of-hope autographs in the senior class picture section.

There he was, her first love, smiling up at her from over forty years ago, frozen in black and white, forever young. She touched the picture, running her finger across his cheek. With a quirky smile and a dimple in Chuck's left cheek, no wonder she was a sucker for CJ's dimple.

Chuck had written, "I wish you love."

Dear Lord, where was Chuck now? Was he all right? Did he ever think about her?

CJ peered over her shoulder at the open page. He took the book away from her, laid it down, and pulled her to him. They began dancing to the soft rock-and-roll waltz of an unchained melody, timeless and forever. When the song faded, her serene smile invited him to kiss her. He did, with

255

infinite tenderness.

Still in his embrace, she looked up at him. "Thank you, CJ, for being here for me. I don't mean to turn all frilly and get the maudlin weepies, but it's been a hard couple of days for me. Tonight was a real zinger."

"Maggie, come."

"Uh-oh! Lord! Now what?" She breathed the prayer as CJ directed her over to the loveseat.

Sitting sideways and facing her, he took both of her hands in his. "What is your full name?"

"Maggie ... Maggie Storm Blue. Why?"

Reacting to her answer, CJ looked somewhere between thunderstruck and dumbfounded. Again, she wondered why.

"The whole time you've been here, I never heard your full name. Stupid me, I never asked, either. I was wrapped up in getting to know you better. When I saw your picture in the yearbook just now ..." His voice trailed off. He cleared his throat and took a deep breath.

"The other day, when we were cruising through Augusta, I told you about a girl that I'd lost many years ago through my own carelessness. Tonight, when you sang *Cruel War*?" He drew in another deep breath, exhaled and paused. "Your high school minstrel show, senior year, you sang that in a guitar duet with another gal, right?"

Maggie scowled, mystified. "Ye-es. But how did you know about that?"

"You wrote to me, all excited. Because yours was one of the few acts chosen to play in a special concert at the Veterans Hospital in Togus. And your duet received a standing ovation from the veterans."

Now it was her turn to be dumbstruck. She grabbed onto the first part of his statement and stuttered, "I wrote to *you*?"

His brown eyes reflected gentleness and wonder. "Your silver pen, upstairs? I recognized it, *mi corazón*. I gave it to you for graduation. The other night, when you told me the story behind it, I was stunned that you still had it. You are the woman I searched for. You are *my* Maggie."

"B-but you can't be him," she sputtered, confused. "His name was Charles, Chuck, but—"

"Maggie Storm Blue, hush. Listen to me." He tapped two fingers on her lips, shushing her. "Colin Jesse Dubois is my *real* name. When I was ten years old, my stepfather murdered my mother. I was the only witness. To keep me under the radar until he was executed, my foster parents changed my name to Charles Wood. You guessed it – my nickname was 'Woodchuck,' which I hated. Right before I moved to Texas and got married, I had my name changed legally, back to my birth name."

No wonder she hadn't put the pieces together. Time! Same face, grown older, only the name was different. *Yeowser!*

"Now what, Lord?" she whispered.

"Listen, Child," came the answer.

"CJ. I-I …"

"Hush, my Maggie." He placed his hands on each side of her face and lowered his to meet hers. Their lips touched like a whisper then went eloquently deeper.

Maggie remembered a certain moonlit night in a long-ago April, standing with a young man under the boughs of an oak tree.

"Oh, my!" she gasped.

Their foreheads touched.

"I know, Maggie mine."

Maggie leaned back on the soft loveseat, still holding CJ's hand.

Okay, seriously, Lord, now what?

However, she wasn't sure she wanted to know. She had been through a lot, these past years and this past month, week, and today. Shaken, yes, but she was still standing.

CJ, looking a little stunned himself, beamed just like he'd just won the lottery.

Skittish about trekking along any more dusty roads of memory tonight, needing an emotional vacation for a few hundred years, and not knowing what else to do, Maggie changed the subject.

"Tomorrow I'm going home, to a job that I now know I hate. Distance always provides a far better perspective. My heart is here in Baysinger Cove. In more ways than you know. Well, maybe *you* do," she said, patting his hand. "My darling relatives have given me an offer I shouldn't refuse, but one that must be put in reserve, for now. Can you envision the horns of this dilemma I'm facing?"

"Yes, I see it, Maggie. It takes you time to come to a decision, and there's no shaking you loose when you finally decide, right?"

She nodded, idly tracing the veins on the back of the hand holding hers. *Three weeks he'd known me − am I that transparent? Check that! Forty-some-odd years ago! We've so much to catch up on.*

"Cuando quiera, donde quiera, como quiera, querida,"

he murmured against her cheek. "Anytime, anywhere, anyhow, my love," he translated, "always, Maggie, my love, *mi corazón*. I am not going to lose you again."

"You won't, CJ. You won't."

In the background, Charlie Rich was bemoaning the woes of searching for the most beautiful girl in the world. CJ disagreed, and told Maggie why, because he wasn't searching any longer.

After a short interlude, CJ leaned back on the loveseat with Maggie's head resting on his shoulder. "Tomorrow, we're going on the same flight, so leaving here won't be quite so hard on you or your folks."

"That's what you think."

"You're next to a window, and I'm in the seat beside you."

At that statement, she sat straight up and said, "How'd you manage that? I'm flying coach and seat preferences are not guaranteed. It's nearly impossible to convince airlines to switch people around."

CJ laughed and kissed her hand. "Coach? No, *querida*, we're both in first class. At six-four, Maggie mine, there is no other way I'll fly."

The End? No! It's really just the beginning. Stay in touch!

Pearls

What images do we conjure up when we hear the word? Is it the Pearl of the Orient, or perhaps the pearl of great price that is mentioned in the Bible? The word itself has become a metaphor for things rare, fine, and valuable. It is the gem birthstone for June.

Pearls have enjoyed a history spanning thousands of years. As far back as 4200 BC, Egyptians used mother-of-pearl for decorations. Roman women in the first century BC sewed so many pearls on their gowns that they walked on the pearl-encrusted hems.

Pearls are "nacre," created when a grain of sand or other irritant finds its way into the shelled mollusk's soft tissue, specifically its mantle. They are made up of calcium carbonate in minute crystalline form, deposited in concentric layers. The ideal pearl is perfectly round and smooth. Baroque pearls are oddly shaped.

Cultured pearls are farm raised. Dedicated workers install a tiny, symmetrical irritant into each oyster, thereby harvesting pearls that are round and of more value than their freshwater cousins. Freshwater pearls come from freshwater mollusks, and are usually irregularly shaped.

The most valuable pearls are wild pearls. They occur spontaneously in the wild and are extremely rare.

Whether wild or cultured, gem quality pearls are nacreous and iridescent like the interior of the shells that produce them. Colors may be white, cream, yellow, brown, green, blue, pink, silver, black, or rainbow.

Imitation pearls, made of glass, are used in costume jewelry and are easily distinguished from genuine pearls. Plastic craft pearls are very lightweight and often adorn felt calendars, inexpensive clothing, and children's crafts.

"Uncultured Pearl" as used in the book's title, refers to a coarseness of manner or morals, namely Robert Morgan and Victor Turner.

Sherrill uses the elongated rice-shaped pearls, either craft or freshwater, for flower petals or other seam treatment adornments on her crazy quilts.

The Author

Sherrill M. Lewis is a self-taught artist across diverse media. Since her senior year in high school, she has won awards for writing, art dolls, beadwork, crazy quilts, and photography. In 2010, her first technique-oriented book, *Splendiferous Bead Motifs!*, was published. Raised in Maine, she currently resides on an idyllic, never boring, five acres in Payne County, Oklahoma, with her husband Gene.

Photo by Karen Lemley © 2003

Made in the USA
San Bernardino, CA
16 October 2014